TOTAL QUEST

Total VR: 1 an MMORPG Story
By Clay Griggs

ACKNOWLEDGEMENTS

To my girls Simone and Octavia.

To my big bro, sis, Mom, and Dad

Special thanks to:
Bob Griggs
my betas
https://www.facebook.com/groups/LitRPGsociety/

This is a work of fiction. Names, characters, places, things, ideas and incidents and happenings are products of the author's imagination and/or are used fictitiously. Any similarity to actual persons, organizations, and/or events, names, characters, places, things, ideas and incidents and happenings is purely coincidental.

Cover art provided by Simone Griggs

Table of Contents

TOTAL QUEST

PROLOGUE

"Alphy, duck!" Panic shrieked as she swept her massive black greatsword toward his head. "Shit!" he said, as he bent his knees, and tucked into a curl. The huge ogre had immobilized him from behind with a bear hug and tightened his arms around Alphy. The tuck caused the ogre to lift back in reflex, raising his head and opening his neck to Panic's swing. The air brushed the back of Alphy's hair and neck as the blade passed over. He heard a wet *thwack!* Hot, sticky liquid splattered down his neck and back. The ogres head bounced off the back of his and rolled into his view. Alphy chuckled. "Ah, a real bloodbath, yeah? I could have taken him..." The game's level alert prompted like mystical wind chimes.

"Lili, show most recent progression stats." Alphy said.

"Opened." His AGI (artificial gaming intelligence) Lili replied. The dialogue opened in his view and he glanced over it as Lili read it aloud:

"You hit ogre for 100 damage. You hit ogre for 100 damage. You kill ogre for 10 experience. You hit ogre for 100 damage. Ogre Bear Hugs you. You are immobilized. Ogre squeezes you for 100 damage. Ogre squeezes you for 100 damage. Panic hits ogre for 100 damage. Panic inflicts critical hit for 300 damage. Panic decapitates ogre for Instant kill. You gain 10 experience. You gain group bonus 240 experience. You gain Ogre Slayer badge. Welcome to level fifty."

"Okay." He said, "Close it back up."

That was the last ogre in the jungle camp. In this beta version of the game Total VR, the average ogre NPC (non-player character) measured in at two meters, two hundred kilograms of muscle and fat. Fleshy, hairless monsters with flat, round teeth, they would often gather in small groups to graze on the local fauna and flora. When they ate everything in the area, they would move the camp on to new feeding grounds. Knocking out ogre camps was not only a good challenge for high-level players, but also helped the lower-level players by keeping low-level NPCs around for them to kill for XP (experience points). Panic and Alphy had been taking out ogre camps for the last few hours. The beta rewarded groups by doubling experience gained at the end of an encounter with a group bonus. Already maxed at level fifty the game still kept track of their experience. If the beta had more levels unlocked they would both be around level eighty.

They'd found this camp high in the hilly jungle area on the east side of the map. These ogre SOBs were playing a game of stone toss when they got jumped by the two players. The ogre's headless body, squirting blood from its clean decapitation, still clung to Alphy in a tight bear hug. He glanced around, then asked, "That's good, yeah? I just received the Ogre Slayer badge with that one! How many ogre's does that make now?" Waiting for Panic to answer, he pried at the fingers and hands still clasping him. His energy was drained; only five percent left. Better to pry the headless ogre off manually than use the last of his energy to explode the clinging arms. Panic flicked the blood from her blade, she answered in her South Indian English, "Badge? Well, if you just received the Ogre Slayer badge, it would be five hundred. You should have an extra ten percent damage increase when fighting ogres." She continued to clean the blade with a rag she plucked from the ground.

Alphy wriggled, breaking free with a strained "Argh!" The ogre's body thumped to the ground. Alphy grimaced, and wiped at the back of his head and neck, smearing more than cleaning the sticky drying blood and pieces of dirt and flesh. They had made a wonderful mess. Littered about them and on them, the gore of two dozen ogre bodies slowly soaked into the environment. It would take about two hours. The ogres would respawn eat whatever was around then find a new area to set up their camp.

"When you gonna come to the island and say hello? I got friends with a beach house on North Shore," Alphy said as he began to auto-loot his share of the corpses. A massive amount of loot from the twenty-four dead bodies flooded his inventory. "Lili, trash anything not rare or craft material."

"Oh, Alphy. Probably never. I can hardly support myself now in the little studio. I can't afford a ticket to Hawaii. You come to Texas!" Panic was more selective, picking through the available treasures—displayed as spectral name tagged objects floating above the bodies—she looted an Ogre Tooth. This was a decent crafting item. She voice-activated her AGI interface. "Coolsans, open inventory." A window opened before her like a spreadsheet. Never happy with the low quality of standard options, she had customized her inventory by every cross-reference she could think of. "Put this in Crafting under Teeth." She tossed the tooth in front of her, and it fell into its proper place. "Close," she said, and the inventory disappeared. Auto-looting, the way Alphy did, wasn't nearly as efficient in terms of categorization of items and usage. Everything just got picked up and dumped into your immediate inventory slots, too much like a garbage heap of items.

Panic and Alpha Beta had never meet in RL (real life), but they'd been the best of friends since Total Quest Beta launched over a year ago. They had grouped together on the first day to attack a prairie beast. Both were trying to complete the same quest and needed meat to turn in to the NPC that offered task to the players. By the time they dropped the beast, Panic had resorted to calling him Alphy and they had both dinged level three, together ever since. And now, after building up their characters and their friendship for over a year of online beta testing Total Quest, the final hours of this unique world were winding down.

Panic was a warrior class player. She stood at the max height of 190 centimeters and ninety kilograms, all rippling muscle, like an Olympic athlete. Her gear was an eclectic ensemble of leather and spiked metal leaf fashioned into an unconventional bikini rated as Heavy Armor. Alphy was a cleric class player, 170 centimeters and eighty kilograms of lean muscle. He had on a leather kilt and vest fashioned like a

Roman sentinel, but it made Alphy look like a Koa warrior from the islands. The game mechanics based the avatar's face on the players that created them. A kukui wood relic hung around his neck. It increased his cleric skills with a sweet plus fifty percent to critical chance. He carried no weapons—clerics rarely used them, as grappling was their primary fighting skill and healing their primary role.

"Alphy, this was a good idea." She was beaming, hungry for more. Together they were a formidable duo, but with their other friend, a mage named Fatal, they ruled the beta.

"What a way to end a great beta game," he said. "Oh, man! Remember the first time you told me to duck?" He cackled as he grabbed his neck.

Her face reddened at the memory of decapitating him. She held back the laughter but a snort escaped. "Oh yeah. Your eyes got so big when you saw the blade coming for you! Didn't I knock your head over a stream?" She covered her laughs with curled fists, but the memory of his face when she followed through with the blade caused her to laugh even harder.

He grunted. "I don't know; I was dead. I doubt you could have hit my head so far. Everyone says I have a big head, yeah?"

She let her smile fade as she furrowed her brow. "I wish we weren't going to lose all our progress, all of our equipment." She held up the greatsword. It was her favorite, earned after many months of grueling quests and crafting. She had forged it with black steel, and gave it a razor-sharp double-edged blade. The blue edges gleamed at the smallest hint of light, and the hilt was a dark blue leather made from narwhal hide. Even with the weight, the balance made it easy for her to twirl it around like a toy. One of the allures of the game was its demand on the physical training of the player. The warrior and cleric classes were especially physically demanding. As new skills are unlocked to the player, they player has to physically perform the skill to a satisfactory proficiency before it levels. Panic in the real world had become quite experienced as a swords woman, though she might not have recognized it. The game had made both of them physically fit as athletes.

Panic did a few of her sword forms. Falling into the playful Cat Paw, she swatted down from an overhead swing with the flat of the blade. From Cat Paw she coiled herself, pulling back into Viper Strike and exploding into a forward lunge. She marched three steps forward, swinging figure eights of Infinity Dips, then about-faced and squatted down, flipping the great blade over and behind her back as a shielding pose Turtle Shell. She looked over at Alphy. He was gawking at her, as usual.

"You like to watch me practice, Alphy?" She snickered.

"Nah, I'm just waiting to see you slip up and fall on your butt."

"When beta ends"—she kept swinging— "our gear... our maps"—she spun the blade over her head in Maple Seed Falling— "all our skill sets, gone..." She took in a deep breath and sighed. "You want to call it quits?" she asked with a mighty down-thrust of the sword with Chopping Wood. "I need to go to bed soon anyways. I have work in the morning."

Alpha Beta shook his head. "What? No. I thought you had tomorrow off so we could play all night, until they unplug it at midnight."

"I did! I requested the day off two months ago, when Total Quest announced the end date of the beta." She sheathed her blade on her back. "They gave it to me, but yesterday my manager said I had to work or lose my job. You know I have to be a model employee. I need that job."

"I would just quit..." he mumbled.

"I want to, but I can't." She took in a long breath. "They expect massive response from the people who preordered for pick-up, plus all the last-minute shoppers. This is worse than Christmas or Black Friday. We have over two thousand deluxe packages on the sales floor, ready to go."

"Dang, that's a lot of game systems."

"Tomorrow will be a very long day."

"Hey." He walked over to her and patted her on the shoulder. "You and me and Fatal, we are top of our class. I'm the best damn cleric, and you're the best damn warrior. We should go down with the ship." He smeared blood on her cheek and smirked.

She glowered at him rubbing her thumb at the fresh gore on her face. "What do you mean, down with the ship?"

Alphy shrugged. "You know... play the game until they unplug the network... kill the beta. You know?"

Panic nodded. "Yeah! You're right, Alphy. I can't believe I have to work tomorrow. It's so unfair. Those bastards, those money-hungry bastards..."

Alphy reached up and pulled her in with one arm. "Come on, let's go kill a big boss. Think how good you will feel after that, yeah? Killing a big, bad boss? You can sleep it off at work tomorrow."

The lust for blood sparkled in her eyes again, the war beast awakened once more. "Yes. Let's do it!"

Panic fluttered her hands, opening chat channels, and created a raid party yet to be filled. Alphy accepted his invite, but his heart sank. She had invited everybody. Fatal accepted the invite and joined them on the command channel.

"Panic? Alpha Beta?" Fatal said. "Where are we going and what are we gonna kill?"

"Alphy and I are working our way down from the jungle to the Southern Canyons in the maps center," she said. "We'll meet you there."

"Great, I'll start there now," he replied.

Alphy scratched at his chin. "You want to kill the King Crocotta?"

"Yeah, he's the biggest boss." A sinister scowl was on her face.

"Well, we need a huge party for that..." Alphy said.

Panic didn't respond, but bounded away down the hilly, thickly forested area, jumping and running through the vines and ferns of the jungle. As usual, he followed her like a puppy.

The beta map was one huge island. It was bordered north and south with coastal beaches and cliffs overlooking the sea. East and west borders were mountainous regions, snow- and ice-themed on the west mountains, and the east, where they were, was filled with thick jungle. The southern coast dropped off into the sea with cliffs overlooking the ocean. Players making their way north from the south end would pass through barren deserts with dunes and eventually, in the middle of the map, deep canyons. The canyons gradually disappeared into the north as the grasslands continued to the only player town on the map. The grassland stopped turned into rolling beaches for about half a kilometer until the sea claimed the border.

They skipped any mob (roving NPCs that would engage them in battle) on their journey to the canyons, as they made their way down the jungle hills and ventured west toward grassland.

"Are you sure you want to do a big raid?" Alphy asked.

"Of course," Panic replied. "I want to kill King Crocotta. He's the toughest fight on the island. Plus, his death re-spawns all the cool-down markers of the lesser bosses. After that we can take on some smaller bosses until game ends." As they ran out into the grasslands, Panic stopped, looking around.

"Wow, it's so beautiful here. Just like your home?" she asked.

"This place is so much like my island it's creepy," Alphy mumbled.

Panic laughed. "A beautiful place to be trapped, Alphy."

"You know, Panic," Alphy continued, "I have never left my island my entire life. Even this game, it's the same for me. No escape."

"I don't know, Alphy. I would rather struggle in paradise than in the mundane."

They kept running through the softly burrowed soil and clumps of grasses and shrubs as canyons began to groove deeply into the ground before them. Herds of grazing prairie beasts darted about, calling out warnings as the players ran near. Panic was not interested in them today. But they did drop high-quality steaks if you could take them down quickly enough. The longer a player battled a prairie beast, the more the quality of the meat would decrease. The ground gouged out before them into old river beds and crags.

"Here we are." Panic thrust her sword into the air victoriously. "Crocotta Canyon." She cheered as she slowed to a brisk walk. A crocotta was a doglike beast with cloven feet and a humanoid face. They frequently associated with goblins and hyenas.

"Fatal, we're ready," Panic said.

"Almost there," Fatal replied. "Alpha Beta, you good?"

"Yeah, great." Alphy forced his top lip up into a mock smile. He had planned on spending these last few hours alone with her. He was miserable, but added, "I'm glad we get to keep our names and our AGI for the new game. I would hate to have to find you all over again and reinitialize with a new AGI interface. I like Lili. It would feel so weird."

Panic shook her head. "Nah, I don't think it would be that big of a deal. The AGIs seem to be interchangeable, don't they? The way you describe your AGI, Lili sounds just like my Coolsans. A simple form of intelligent game interface is all they are, like a smart phone." She paused. "You're right. I would hate to use your phone. What a mess. I would have to repeat the personalization of my entire interface..." She reared her fist back and punched him in the shoulder so hard that he flew a few meters before hitting the ground. "Let's kick King Crocotta's butt!" She swung her greatsword with the forms Maple Seed Falls then Chopping Wood. With a grin, Alphy looked up and sighed, watching her move.

The mass invite was sent to all the beta players, along with an invite to the raid group. Panic divided them into the only three classes in the game, warrior, cleric, and mage. Fatal would lead the mages, Panic the warriors, and Alpha Beta the battle support clerics. Each group had a dedicated battle speak or chat channel, the three commanders connected with command chat. With a large mixed entourage of players, Fatal and company mustered around Alphy and Panic.

"Fatal," Panic squeaked, "I am so glad you made it. Alphy talked me into staying up late."

"Good job, Alpha Beta," Fatal said. "It wouldn't be as fun without you, Panic."

"Hmph," Alphy replied. "I know; her boss gave her the day off, then threatened her job if she didn't come in."

"Okay, enough of my job," Panic said. "Do you two have your groups set to go?"

"Yeah, I think I have about four-hundred mages," Fatal said. "The battle channel is good to go."

"Clerics are ready too, three hundred'ish." Alphy replied. "I'll told them to find a few battle buddies to keep an eye on."

"Okay, then," she said. "My warriors are all set around six hundred. Set battle chats to speaker, then we can hear each other's commands."

In her top-right view, Panic had six ten-by-ten grids of the warriors in her battle group. Each name had a red and blue column under it. As the players would use health or energy, the colors would lower in the column, red for health and blue for energy. Fatal and Panic had similar displays of their subordinates.

"Okay, Alphy, smash the goblin totem!" Panic said.

Planted to the side of the path was the goblin totem that triggered the King Crocotta event upon its destruction. Alphy crushed it with his boot and all the players cheered as a map wide warning glared in everyone's view "King Crocotta has been activated." Almost every beta player had shown up, covering the canyon trail with teeming numbers of metal, skin, and gleaming weaponry. This was a sexy game, and as such, all the players could show as much skin as they desired. Ripped six-pack abs, lean and bulky arms and legs, all of it stuffed into tight, low-cut tops and cleavage-showcasing armor. The clerics had cargo pockets on everything: miniskirts, kilts, traditional cargo pants, A-shirts, T-shirts, or just a tight open vest with one strained button holding it closed—with pockets, of course. Everyone looked like they were dressed for a cosplay party on the beach. Even the mages wore one-piece corsets, bikini battle suits, or leaf-plate kilts under their robes. Exposing the flesh allowed for blades, claws, and teeth to leave the scars of battle. Scars of battle accentuated the players' notoriety. At least, that was the reason Total Quest gave for the racy style and fashion of the game.

"Okay, people," Panic shouted, "this is our last beta raid. We have spent months and months making ourselves awesome. Let's bathe in the blood of our enemies!" Hundreds of voices went up in cheers and yells. A deep growl joined the joyous celebrants. The AGI running this area of the map would scale events based on total player presence. With such a huge turnout, it had doubled the usual size of the King Crocotta, spawning it at an enormous ten meters tall. This dog beast with hooves and a creepy, humanlike face stretched its jaws wide in a reverberating howl, drowning out the cheers and cries of the players.

From where they had gathered at the entrance to a long, straight, deep canyon, the players looked up to the other side. The boss had a guard spawning around it: several hundred rusty-brown furred crocotta mingled with hundreds of green-skinned goblins and patchy black-and-grey-coated hyenas. As if the ground itself was giving birth to the beasts, they rippled out around King Crocotta. As it roared, the monster army began its advance down into the canyon, down on the players. As Panic had desired, the slaughter began. The beasts charged down from ledges into the canyon, yipping, barking, and jeering at the players. By the hundreds they charged and crashed into the gleaming line of armor-plated warriors and swirling great swords, war hammers, and battle-axes.

Player and monster alike fell as a dark red mist rose from the field. The warriors forced a front line by Panic's command and began a slow drive forward. Alpha Beta signaled his clerics to move into a support position behind the warriors. Clerics were lightly armored, but the lack of durability was made up for with high agility and speed. They were grapplers with amazing DPS against one or two opponents. Clerics needed to make physical contact with their foe for maximum DPS.

As the warriors hacked and sliced, the clerics dove in and out of the fray, using their Rupture ability to rip deadly tears into the monsters as they touched them. Another huge wave followed a great, roaring bellow from the king, and a second wave of fur and green skin charged down into the canyon, hundreds and hundreds more. The mages twirled and waved their wands, scepters, and staffs, crafting and weaving their spells.

Fatal commanded in a loud, booming voice, "Purple Nurple to the fore; Static ten meters beyond!" and with that, great surges of purple and green power stretched from their instruments of focus. The globular energy swirled and clawed forward on the surface of the ground, tearing its way through the lines of clerics and warriors, withholding destruction for the line of monsters. There, all forms of purple hell exploded.

The Purple Nurple spell crawled up the legs of the crocotta goblins and hyena, exploding small circles of flesh into vapor. This left the first line hemorrhaging and. As the purple energy began to snap back to their owners' tools of focus, the green Static began setting its trap for the next surge pushing down into the canyon. Fatal watched the grid of players under his control, keeping an eye on the energy point consumption. Purple Nurple was cheap for EP and had a decent damage output. Looking at the battle statistics Purple Nurple took ten percent of the targets health, pulled five percent of the average energy point or EP total, but the energy refresh was around ten percent per second. It was like shooting a pistol with unending rounds. It wasn't as powerful as a shot gun, but over time it would still do the job.

Canyon wall to canyon wall, the Static spell snared and attached a condition that dramatically slowed movement of the assaulting force. Clinging to any enemy that touched the surface of the ground, it reduced the charge to a stop, causing a collision of monsters to pile upon themselves. The back line still rushed forward, forcing and shoving with momentum and rage into the hobbled mess before them. The warriors and clerics finished off the beasts in front of them, causing swift end to the victims of Purple Nurple. The air was full of level alerts, chiming the signal for player advancement as monster bodies piled up. "Forward!" Panic called, and the line of warriors advanced to the Green Static line. The slaughter, the feel of blade tugging, ripping flesh, the splatter of blood and flicked sweat, the smell of the animals, beasts, and humans filled Panic with fuel. Adrenaline surged through her body.

Fatal pulled free a sheathed greatsword strapped to his back. He swept the weapon made of bone and ridged with teeth through the air as he commanded, "Battle mage, freestyle!" Several hundred mages drew their greatswords and began swirling them in the air over their heads. The swords began to hum and chirp as they charged up energy in various colors. The battle mages' attack with their greatswords produced a devastating blow to an enemy, but lost the safety of a ranged attack.

The warriors had beaten down the first several lines of monsters as they stomped over the fallen beasts. The king was in sight now. "Break their lines!" Panic howled, and the warriors surged forward into the king's guard as their flanks came under attack by the remaining monster army. King Crocotta, towering at the height of the canyon, howled again, looking down at them. Alpha Beta commanded the clerics to alternate between Rupture on the monsters and Mend on their allies. Rupture would vibrate a target out of alignment, causing wounds; Mend vibrated the target into alignment, healing wounds.

King Crocotta let out a mighty growl, sending the remainder of his minions down into the slaughter. The battle mages rushed to the front alongside the warriors. Players began to fall with the increased pressure of the king's guard. Alpha Beta called, "Clerics focus on mending the battle mage! Their health is dropping! The warriors can take it." The far rear line of mages continued the assault casting Purple

Nurple, helping the front line by cleaning up the peripheral monsters. The clerics rushed forward, healing the battle mages as quickly as they could, but the King Crocotta attacks were AOE (area of effect) and very powerful. Players were falling faster than they could be healed. But they had the numbers to win, and they knew it. The raid pressed on. King Crocotta howled and bellowed, cussing and spitting at the battle mages and clerics. Dropping his front hooves down on the players, he triggered his Sonic Blast skill. Unblockable and devastating, it depleted the life points of the battle mages in a five-meter radius. The clerics in the area were just as vulnerable and were lost on the attack. Panic watched the grid as two solid blocks of one hundred fell by seventy five percent HP. Without clerics healing a second blast might take out the remaining force. She glanced at the complete player raid grid. She was down three-hundred warriors, Fatal was alive and had two-hundred mages left at an average of fifty percent health, Alphy was doing great hardly any HP lost but his clerics had taken a beating with the Sonic Blast. The cleric force was down by two-hundred. They had to do this quick or it wasn't going to work.

The back line of clerics breached and began pulling casualties to safe distance for healing. Panic yelled "Warriors swarm!" and the warriors stepped in to finish the beast off. Fatal croaked in a raspy voice, "Static!" and the remaining mages focused green static energy from scepter and greatsword, snaring King Crocotta for a few moments. In the few seconds Static held the king, warriors hacked with greatswords and battle-axes, and crushed with war hammers. King Crocotta health bar was down to thirty percent and he was immobilized by Static. The rear haunches of the great beast gave out as the king fell to its hind legs. It howled and bellowed, lifting its great front hooves, smashing them down on unfortunate players and sending out another Sonic Blast. Seeing the great hooves being raised, most of the players rolled and dodged out of the way. Still it dropped many more of the assaulting force, leaving only a few hundred mages and clerics alive. The warriors left, about three-hundred, had a higher HP count; most had at least twenty five percent HP left. "Now!" Panic cried. "Special attacks." Each player in the game had a special attack; the only similarity of a player's special attack was that it generally increased damage output by a considerable amount, but was usable only every few hours due to cool down. The surviving warriors, clerics, and mages all hit King Crocotta at the same time with their special high-DPS attacks, clerics squeezing through to contact the rear haunches of the beast. The Beasts health bar flashed red and fell to one percent.

It was glorious. King Crocotta dropped its jaws, straining to stand on its front legs as players teemed around him like maggots devouring a carcass. Howling, King Crocotta lashed out its massive front hooves again, but the attack was weak. The players' special DPS strike ripped through the beast, shaking it violently as its head exploded. A rain of carnage and loot fell down from the defeated beast, showering the players in the blood and pieces of flesh and fur. A monstrous clash of cymbals sounded as fireworks erupted with great booms in the sky above them. The players cheered in delight as they swarmed over the loot falling on the ground all around them. The remaining mobs scattered, returning to previous scripted routes and priorities; a few of the players sent ranged attacks, and some chased them down to finish them off. Within the rain of blood and gore, instruments of war, crafting supplies, all kinds of rare and exotic loot fell for the victors. Clerics began healing the fallen as others rushed about eagerly, seeing what loot they'd earned.

All three of the friends, Panic, Alpha Beta, and Fatal, had survived the battle. Fatal walked over, a grand smile stretched across his face, laying hands on his friends' shoulders he said "A glorious beginning to our unfortunate end. We need to meet up in the new world to celebrate." Panic and Alpha Beta nodded in agreement. Alpha Beta added, "We could start on launch day and go from there."

Panic backhanded Alphy in the gut and said, "Hey, I have to work, remember?"

Alphy paled. "Oh, sorry... forgot."

Fatal interjected, "How about we just wait for Panic? That will be the start date for us. Any way we do it, I've been thinking about this for a few days. We call our party Trinity Ball or Trinity Festival or something like that. You know? We show up every few weeks and trigger map bosses for raid events. We're the best of the three classes. We can lead the charts in the new game. Maybe even start a guild or clan if that's an option. But we wait for Panic."

Panic smiled at them both. "You would wait for me? I love you guys. Let's do it!"

"I don't know, Fatal," Alphy said. "I really want to play on launch day." He kept his eyes from Panic while saying this. He couldn't help but fidget with his wooden relic. Pinching his chin, Panic pulled his face up and curled up one side of her mouth. "It's okay, Alphy. It isn't fair to make you suffer just because I have to work. But let's start the Trinity bash when I can return to the game to play. Deal?" She crisscrossed her arms in front of herself, hands sticking out, the other two did the same, and they shook on it, three ways.

"Well, I'm not done tonight. See you two squares in the new world," Fatal said while turning away. He shouted, "I'm leading a raid to sweep from south up on the west side of the map. Whoever wants to join, let's go!" And off Fatal went, with a large trail of mixed-class players following him.

Bombastic, a small female mage, called out, "I'm gonna sweep up from the east through the jungles and on to the north beach for a party." A great cheer went up from the players. "Well?" she said. "Let's go!" A massive group formed with her, and they broke away down to the southeast.

"Come on, Alphy, we can take center," Panic said.

"Yeah, sure," Alphy replied. "We gonna bring the rest of these spare wheels with us?" He thumbed at the other players. Their eyes filled with as much eagerness as Panic's.

"Of course." She thrust her sword into the air. "Let's move out!" The remnants of the raid party all cheered as they set off to the south boundary cliffs. The raid chat was still on, and Bombastic was added to command chat. The players all agreed to kill-sweep all the way back to the north shore for a final beach party.

Hours passed in game, and the players cleaned the island to the bone, not one boss left alive. Slowly, a great beach party began to grow on the north shore as teams of players rolled in. The day had passed into the dark evening; the end of the game swiftly approached. The friends sat around a large bonfire, watching as the ocean breezes played with the dancing embers rising far above their heads.

Panic mumbled, "I wish you lived in Texas, Alphy. I could use a friend to cry on after work tomorrow." The massive purge they'd played on the island, the last hours of the game spent, had made her maudlin. More players, still online, gathered on the beach. They would all go down with the ship, gathered together on the north shore.

There were only a few minutes left. Bonfires littered the beach as they waited for the end of the beta. Panic sighed. "I know I won't be able to play for a few days. I'll be too tired from work." She took a deep breath. "When I log back in, I want to be ready."

"For what, Panic?" Alphy asked.

"To win, to be the best again, to fight and sweat."

Alphy patted her on the head.

"Thanks for talking me into staying online, Alphy."

He turned his head and studied her face for a moment, then hesitantly said, "Sure. I wish I lived in Texas too. I hate where I live. It's just like here. A tiny green island in the middle of an endless sea. It's claustrophobic and it's so hot all the time. I fill buckets with sweat. I used to go to Costco with my mom so I could stand in the dairy freezer to cool down."

He was trying for a bit of sympathy, but Panic started giggling at him. "Oh, Alphy, you're always so funny."

Alphy scrunched his face in hurt confusion. He never understood why she always laughed at him when he shared his emotions, but he did like to see her happy. Her laugh was contagious, and he soon joined. The sun set behind the mountains to the west, a last brilliant display of purples, blues, and reds before the world turned black.

1: PAID TO PLAY

Fatal found himself looking out over the sea of the southern player boundary; he allowed himself to dive into melancholy. Defeating the King Crocotta had created an emptiness, a suffocating lump in his chest. He pondered the idea of emptiness causing a blockage. An endless fall into thick darkness.

"I hate endings..." he mumbled. He zapped a full charge of Lightning to the sea. *Crack!*

"They totally suck," he heard a husky female voice reply. He didn't bother looking up. Hundreds of other players gathered about him were checking their gear and inventories for the final kill sweep up the west side of the map.

"Yeah, so sad they make me want to cry," another female voice, sharper higher pitched, replied.

"It doesn't matter how they fix their gear. It's all over." Fatal sighed, "I wish we never had to leave. I know the new world will be cool, but I built all my stats into Purple. I'm gonna have to start from scratch. It's not fair."

He felt fingers gently sliding up the back of his head, softly scratching him behind his right ear. "You poor little human." He looked to his left for the source of this strange yet agreeable comfort. The husky voice, a red-haired warrior stood with a sly grin as she continued to pacify him like a puppy. It worked—he liked it.

"Cherry, you can't have everybody." Shrieked the other one. Fatal felt a tug on his right arm and turned to find a pink-haired warrior looking up at him.

"What?" He felt awkward now. "What's going on?"

The two women burst out laughing, stepping a few steps back, both obviously satisfied and amused.

"That's not cool. I really am upset."

The two warriors ran back into the cluster of prepping gamers, giggling and snickering. He scowled then took in a deep breath.

"Are you all ready yet? Let's do this, we're losing time!" Fatal called out. "We'll do this zerg style! Kill as we go. Don't fall behind, I'm on a timer to reach the beach!" They all roared and cheered and as an angry mob spread like a plague of locusts, everything in their path was destroyed.

They pushed along the sea cliffs toward the mountains. When King Crocotta was defeated, the cool-down on other defeated boss monsters had refreshed. The Ogre Lord, Goblin Gouda, Ice Wendigo Alpha, and Orc Pei were all along the western route, ready to fight.

Ready to fight, that was how he always felt. In the game, at home with his mom—it didn't matter where; he was always ready for a challenge. The only other person he'd met like himself was Panic. She was always looking for blood. Alpha Beta, not so much, Fatal thought Alpha Beta was more in it for Panic than the gameplay. Not Fatal, he loved the action.

They reached the first target on his mental list, the Ogre Lord. They all slowed, seeing the war camp down on the other side of the ridge and waited, ready for his signal.

The Ogre Lord was the only stationary ogre location on the map. Grunt ogres built up a small war camp out of a village in the foothills of the southern mountain ridge. He would only spawn when the war camp was complete. Usual respawn of the war camp was about a week in RL. Ogres would have to rebuild the little fort after each razing the players brought down.

The war camp looked at a hundred percent. The Ogre Lord would be in there. Fatal raised his boney greatsword in the air. All the players lined up to his left and right. They had done this hundreds of times over the last several months.

"When we finish this, we head on to Goblin Gouda. Forget about looting, it doesn't matter anymore. This is about the fight. For each boss we'll line up just like this, so keep up. Good? Everyone ready?"

"We are!" two giggly voices replied.

He looked down the left flank to see the pink-haired girl flailing an arm to show they were ready. They must be sisters in RL or besties.

"Argh!" He thrust his sword forward and charged.

The line descended upon the war camp as stealthily as charging kindergarteners released at recess. However, they still had the ability to Sneak Attack. Ogres were an easy target to sneak up on; they didn't fear much and only paid attention to things when they wanted to eat them. Fatal called, "Shield up!" The mages around him cast shields above their heads as flocks of arrows fell upon them. "Gate!" And like a mass of four-year-old soccer players, they pressed to the gate. "Clerics, Rupture!" Rupture from the force of one-hundred clerics shattered the gate. The durability bar on the massive wooden door dropped to zero in under ten seconds. The warriors streamed in like a floodgate had burst as splintered planks blew in with them. The horns and drums sounded and beat within the walls, alerting every ogre inside of the threat. The system response to Fatal's group attack on the gate allowed the ogre war camp NPCs a Surprise Attack de-buff; this gave all of the ogres minus ten percent on DPS against the players and minus ten percent durability, and gave the players a buff of plus ten percent DPS to the war camp NPCs, plus ten percent durability against the war camp NPCs, a ten percent bonus increase in coinage dropped, and a ten percent increase to experience gained. An area message flashed "Ogre Lord has been activated."

"Bloody slaughterhouse!" the pink-haired girl squealed spinning a dual wield combo of wakizashi swords. Ogres' health bars begun to drop as a red mist enveloped her. She disappeared into the growing mass of fleshy ogres.

"Ow! Ow! Ow!" howled the redhead as she slapped Fatal's ass. Diving into the fleshy horde of ogres she spun a pair of gladius. Pieces of meat and gore flecked his face.

"Hey!" he called after her, but she too disappeared in the immense mess of enraged, de-buffed, and generally pissed off ogres.

"That's my ass..." It was probably a couple of dudes' gender-bending to mess with guys like him. Girls—women never played video games. In fact, he would put one month's paycheck down on the fact Panic was a thirteen-year-old boy. They were messing with his game. Frack it.

"The Ogre Lord! Find the Ogre Lord!" he howled.

By the time tiny prickles of light could be seen on the northern border beach, Fatal and his zerg of players were filthy with blood, dirt, feathers, fur, skin, scales, and a mess of other battle debris. The battle elements' decay would eventually clean them all, but it was much more fun to bathe in the sea. The act carried with it the ritualistic feel of an ancient tradition lost to the ages. An army fresh from the stains of war, renewing and cleansing in the salty sea of purity.

He could be a poet. His mom said he could.

"Hey, everybody." Still on speaker to his group, they could hear him as if he were standing right next to each one of them. "This is such a monumental ending. I have really enjoyed meeting you all over the last year plus. I hope things go well for you all in the new world. I'm still open to hooking up in groups and parties with anyone, so just message me or something after the launch. Okay? Keep an eye out for Trinity. We're going to do this in the new game Total Quest." He felt himself tearing up a little. That hand came back to scratch his ear.

"You are a softy," the redhead said.

"Sweetie, we're gonna take good care of you," Pink Hair said. "It's all gonna be okay. Just wait and see."

"Thanks, guys." He sniffed and turned to the scores of faces looking back at him, just as grief-stricken. "Group Hug!" Fatal yelled.

The entire group of players all stacked onto his position. All of the avatars occupied the same space by using a glitch in the system the players called Group Hug. Somewhere during the beta test, a couple of players pushing the loops and glitches found that if you targeted the leader of a party and rushed in quickly, it wouldn't displace the leader or cause damage to the party. Just meld, without any sensation, graphically overlap. Five seconds later, the system booted everyone but the leader from the space in a player starburst. *Pop!* They all burst out from Fatal, with a promise of continued comradery.

The raid group dwindled down to the beach after Fatal disbanded. Those two crazy women followed him to the fire he reclined at. The pink one sat on his left and the red one on his right, both with mischievous grins. The red one held out her hand.

"I'm Cherry Bomb. You want to get paid to play?"

2: PUPPETEER

Snapper, as the researchers had called him, had been hooked up to a life-support system, body and brain dormant, while his mind was actively commanding monsters to perform a very limited range of attacks against human forces. Unable to use the full extent of his mind, his captors had him hooked on very strong narcotics, and while in the system, they had managed to control and limit his mind with security protocols that clung to him like leeches. In short he was the on demand puppeteer for some crazy VR game. He could barely remember his name, Joseph Turtle.

Some black ops research company—Grey Fifth, was it? He thought that was their name. Memory in and out, all fractured pieces, big chunks and splintered dust, kill the human. The Fifth, or the research doctors, whoever "they" were, had implanted a device into his brain. It didn't hurt, not painful, but he could feel it like a soft wedge touching his awareness, like a cold tab of butter melting into his skin. Working like a key, it unlocked his ability to think, to use his mind, thrusting him from "really smart grad student" to "enlightened Buddha brilliance," That's what he felt like a fucking buddha and that was while he was heavily sedated. The device simply unlocked his mind to full capacity, as if it were the missing link in the human's brain to connect both sides, full enlightenment, the missing puzzle piece of human construction found after a million years of searching. They slid it into his brain just so, and wham, he was complete;

even with his body restrained and tortured, he felt more at peace than when he was free. The universe in its entirety opened inside of his consciousness. That was why they kept him heavily sedated, fogged and fractured, knowing that with a clear and unchained mind, Snapper would be dangerous. That was why they controlled his mental abilities in the physical and in the network.

Complying with their mundane requests did allow his bodily addictions to be sated. Today the research team was about to celebrate the end of the beta, as they called it. The end of the virtual playground he ran around as Snapper, destroying and devouring all he could, anything to quench his appetite. Today they had briefed him for nearly an hour on his "reward": they would let Joseph "the Snapper" Turtle move his consciousness into the virtual environment without any pre-directives, system collars, or restrictions—a real treat.

The drugs only worked on the physical level; when he was in the game, the virtual world, he had no connection to that body, truly separate from that realm until they pulled him back in. The research team had countless security programs and closed network systems within systems when he was released into the beta. The first time he moved into the game, he lost all memory of it upon his return. They had questioned his sedated body for days, but to no avail—nothing recalled. After the second time in, they realized he needed a new form of memory retention to continue progress virtually and physically, back and forth. Memories created in the body were separate from memories attained in the virtual environment. The brain is the human's memory dump, but with the unnatural limitations and restrictions collared on Joseph, he was unable to create a natural connection of his own. He had heard them debating: it was too great a risk, giving him control over his own memories. But there was nowhere for him to store virtual environment experiences without his own connections. It was two worlds with different memory paths and no allowed natural connector. The third time in, they set up a restricted memory dump for him to access when entering and exiting the environment, the back and forth, the to and fro of his body.

Treat time. He had partial access to his mind in here, his clarity felt pure, but he was also aware that they had some control of him. He felt no side effects from the heavy narcotics when he was in virtual reality. Before they launched him into the network, they told him five seconds, only five seconds of freedom until this system was shut down, unplugged for good. The tests had been run for cycles upon cycles and they no longer needed the environment. Time to delete. This was a threat to him—subtle, of course, but he understood. As long as he performed as puppet master for them, he would not be unplugged, terminated.

They launched him into the island (five seconds); it was this environment, mentally cramped as it was, that allowed him to think without the fog of medication in his mind. But when he was set free in the network, he raged with insatiable appetite. To fill, to consume, the hunger was always there. Pushing out, he could feel the sides of the beta map. Escape, but not today, soon enough. A simple solution, as most are. The security walls of the virtual environment were thin even with all the layers the tech crews had caked onto it. He could overload the servers until they lagged and walk out a free man—well... a free mind.

He used a moment to plot his escape; it was afterthought, a natural conclusion, and now he could feast on the NPCs for a few seconds. Reaching out, he devoured beast and monster; without being shoved into an NPC to control like a body puppet, he could simply locate and consume (four seconds). Something different was happening, his attention pulled to the north boundary. He had over four seconds left, an eternity to enjoy. A gathering among humans, tribal bonfires, home... Plenty of time was left to watch the sun setting behind the mountains, feel the warmth of the beach bonfires and the coolness of the ocean waters. He listened to the soft roar of the surf purring onto the beach (three seconds) and the droning hum of people chattering around the pitted blazes (two seconds) before transferring back into his useless husk (.00000001 seconds).

3: ALPHY

When he'd picked Alpha Beta for a gamertag, Margo didn't think it had anything to do with his first name, Alfredo. He never went by Alfredo, always answered to Margo. His mom had told him when he was little that Portuguese pirates had settled on one of the islands, and that was where his name came from, pirate blood. Alphy, Panic always called him that. He liked it. He was thinking about calling himself Alphy now, when meeting new people or when he ran into an old acquaintance. Maybe today he could test it out. Today he would soak his feet in the sand. North shore. Empty beach and cloudy skies, a break from the sun for a few hours. He might get relief with some rain. For now, ankles slowly sinking in the sand, he let the waves beat against his shins. The Beta just ended. The time difference gave him plenty of sun light to enjoy his day off. Over a year of exercise, training in and out of the game and diet change had caused Margo to shed a massive amount of weight in a year's time. He actually got a job last month as a life guard at

Bellows Field Beach Park. He was in great shape, but looked awful.

Plastic surgery, removal of his excess skin, thousands of stitches—if he ever saved up enough money, he could be rid of his deflated body bags. The tide was low, so he flopped on his back, letting it wash over him. So much weight—how did he get so big that he could lose so much weight? If he could blame his family, he wouldn't; no decent food options led families to poor food choices. It was always about money. Everything was about money. The water rushed in, lifting and flapping his folds. He looked like a huge deflated balloon caught on the surf. "Agh!"

Turning his head to the sound of a quad bike, he watched a lifeguard hop down and run to his side. "Oh! You're alive?" He must've been a new life guard, Margo had never seen him before. The man gasped in horror at the site of Margo, or Alphy, whoever he was. Lifting his head, he examined himself, flesh flapping in the receding wave. He turned to the lifeguard and exclaimed, "Oh no! What happened? Is it the jellyfish? Agh!" He held up his arms and flapped them around, spraying water. "Oh, my body is defatting!"

"Oh! Sir, stay calm." Holding his hand out like a cop stopping traffic, the lifeguard called on his radio, "I have a man down, defatting on the beach from jellyfish! What do I do?"

Margo burst out in great, gasping cackles. The water rushed over him, choking his gasps for air. Margo was laughing so hard that he beat the surf and clapped his hands together, howling in delight. The lifeguard called on the radio, "Uh, I think he's in some kind of shock, a seizure or something."

Someone responded on the radio, "Is his skin all floppy and loose? Ask him if his name is Margo."

"Sir?" the young man asked, probably Margo's age, definitely from California, by the accent. "Are you Margo?"

The jig was up. Margo snickered. "Yes." He was still shaking from the well-played joke.

"Yes. It is Margo!" the lifeguard said.

"You have to give him mouth to mouth. It's the only way to reset his breathing rhythm! It's from the long-lung jellyfish sting!" said the operator on the other end, probably Kamalu. "Then you have to pee on him! Now, Chad!"

Margo was rolling back and forth, slapping the ground in hysterics, choking and gasping between bellows. Chad slowly walked over to Margo, unzipping his pants, then catching himself. "Oh, mouth to mouth first." Wide-eyed, he threw himself on Margo and locked lips, blowing as hard as he could.

"Agh!" Margo cried. "That's helping."

Two more quad bikes pulled up—yep, Kamalu on one and Leilani on the other. The two riders hopped off, and Leilani yelled "Chad, you're doing it!" Chad flashed a smile of pride toward her and went back down blowing into Margo's mouth again. "Hey, Chad!" Kamalu said. "He's getting bigger again. Pee on him to stop the poison!" Standing up, Chad grabbed his zipper and said, "This might sting, sir!"

Margo rolled away from Chad and hopped back up. "No, no, bra. I'm good, see?" He flapped his arm skin then smacked his deflated bag of a belly.

Chad eased to a confused smile and said, "Oh, that's good." He nodded. "That's good."

"Hey, Leilani," Margo said, "bonfire today?"

"Yeah, that's cool," she replied. "I'll fire it up around seven, yeah?"

"Thanks, Leilani. I'll bring some fat bombs and rum." With that, the three old friends smiled and confirmed the evening plans as a stunned and confused Chad looked about.

"Should I put up the Jellyfish Warning sign?" he asked. Margo, Kamalu, and Leilani chuckled.

"Hey, Chad, you come over too, yeah? I'll tell you all about the long-lung jellyfish and Margo, he a life guard too!" Leilani chortled and patted Margo on the back as he walked off.

"Hey, call me Alphy," Margo said. "I'm a new person but same old me—whatcha think?"

"I like it, Alphy," Kamalu said.

"Me too. Alphy!" Leilani snickered. Alphy smiled. The island could be big enough sometimes after all.

He went home to pick up his stash of fat bombs—semi-sweet chocolate—and a bottle of clear rum. By the time he showed up at Leilani's bungalow, it was close to dinner. The clouds were hiding from the sun and a nice fire was burning on the beach. There were about twenty people, a mix of old acquaintances and new faces, including the dazed-looking Chad. Alphy set his offering on the rough-cut wooden table that had been carried out to keep the food off the sand. The island wasn't always bad, not during times like this. Leilani hopped over and gave him a big hug.

"Alphy! You want chicken?" She gave her eyebrows a quick waggle.

"Oh, yeah. But you got to try these fat bombs."

"Sure…" She popped one in her mouth then looked up with wide eyes. "Oh, man… That's good. You eat these and lose weight?"

"All about the diet, Leilani." He smiled and looked up to see Chad shyly approaching him. So Alphy gave a friendly wave to the silly Cali guy.

"So, you on Keto or something?" Chad asked.

"Yeah, what you know about that?" Alphy said.

"I did it two years ago, lost a hundred. Should have recognized it when I saw you…" Chad looked down, embarrassed.

"Well, I got to tell you, Chad, you got soft lips."

"Alphy!" Leilani laughed and giggled.

"Oh, uh, Thanks, Alphy," Chad said. "You know, your skin will pull back in a few months to a year. That's when you want to get the surgery."

"What are you talking about?" Alphy asked.

Chad looked at him hard. "You don't want flappy skin, but you should wait at least a year. My aunt works at a clinic in Santa Barbara. The clients that wait do much better."

Alphy smiled. "Hmm, thanks, Hot Lips. I'll think about that."

Chad nodded and walked back to a small group he had been talking to. Leilani greeted some fresh arrivals. Alphy looked around the beach fire and noticed a woman staring at him. When their eyes connected, she formed a satisfied grin on her face. She was a crazy-tall woman dressed in a bikini, her muscles lean and rippled. "Oh, Lordy..." Alphy muttered as the woman stood up and sauntered over to him. She had long, curly, dark hair and tanned olive skin. Her eyelids slightly slanted, framing black eyes with bottomless depths. She stood before him. Alphy looked up; she had to be over six feet easy.

"Hello, cleric. Want to get paid to play the game?" Every consonant pronounced clearly.

"Huh?" He was stunned by her presence, so overwhelming.

"I'm a cleric too. Recruiting for my squad. I want you on it. You'll make a lot of money. Say yes and we can get on with the party."

"Yes..." he said staring into her eyes. He would say anything she wanted. Do whatever she wanted. She was a goddess. Was this Pele come for him? She felt so strong the air seemed to flex around her.

"Here, sign this, then stick your finger in this box... Alphy." She whispered his name with slow intensity, as a thick paper packet and small black box appeared out of nowhere. He signed where she pointed, shoved his finger in the box, and felt a prick at the tip. Gasping, he pulled his finger out with scrunched brow and stared at the droplet of blood that was forming on the tip of his finger. The woman grabbed his hand. He couldn't pull away if he wanted to, but he didn't want to; she could do what she wanted. She brought his finger up to her face, squeezing his finger to pool more blood from the prick.

"Got an ow-y, Alphy?" she whispered with a mocking frown that quickly turned to a wicked grin. "You will address me as Commander, that's my gamertag or Commander Kiri, understand?" She wrapped her lips around his finger, sucking the blood off. He noticed sharp canines and slightly pointed ears. This had to be Pele.

"Uh, yeah. Commander... Uh..."

"Good. Now let's enjoy the party for a few hours. You'll meet a few others in an hour or two."

"Okay..." Alphy's eyes were wide as coconuts and his mouth wouldn't close properly. All he could do, frozen in place, was stare up into her bottomless pits of black.

She grinned and said, "Good. You do what I say when I say it, yes?"

"Yes..."

"I will train you how to be the best you are capable of being. You might even be able to keep up with me and Mortem by the time I'm finished with you, Alphy." She released her firm grip on his hand.

"Oh, you're so strong and tall... are you... are you Pele?" he asked her.

But she burst into laughter "Ha! No, I am not Pele. You are a wise man to compliment your commander so."

"You from Sweden, yeah?"

"Further away than that. Give me a fat bomb; they smell good. I will tell you about the job responsibilities and the required secretive nature of your contract with Griffith." She looked around at the growing party on the beach, fists planted on her hips like Lynda Carter in the old *Wonder Woman* series. She glanced back down at Alphy. "Well? Fat bomb, soldier!"

"Yeah, sure." He smiled back, not sure what had just happened but ready to go with the flow on this one.

4: PANIKAR

She slapped her alarm clock, hand extending out from beneath the mound of wool and cotton she had buried herself under the night before. She hated being cold but, opportunist that she was, loved the right set of circumstances cold weather provided to snuggle under layers of blankets, creating a pocket warmed by her body. Always she had one foot sticking out, like a temperature gauge, keeping the two extremes regulated.

Pulling the wool from her eyes, she blinked away the dream. She had been running with Alphy through a soft, earthen landscape, their heavy combat boots leaving deep prints wherever they trod. The trees and plants in shades of green and blue. Everything strange and familiar. It was some distant planet full of florakin and orcs battling against each other with high-tech weaponry, along with the ancient, traditional tools of war. Alphy and her wielded heavy bolt pistols in one gauntleted hand and sabers in the other, he and she covered with gore and blood. Fighting together against the foe—no memory if it was the orc or florakin they had championed—Alphy and her were victorious, for now, the two survivors of the skirmish. Taking in the tally for the butcher's bill, they stood back to back, gulping raw air thick with cut flesh, burnt flesh, and hair, a brief respite. The battlefield, corpses of both armies littering the ground in clumps...

As she was awakened by the alarm, the dream was cut down like an enemy. It was as real and detailed as any other moment in her day, and quickly it faded to obscurity, leaving her body full of the battle fuel, adrenaline. Shakily, Janus breathed deeply, focusing on her trembling hands, her mind on the day of work that awaited her.

She crawled into the shower. Hot water filled the small stall with steam, melting her cold back in the hot drizzle. She scrubbed away all that remained of the dream, awake and fresh for the day. She would work today as required, then, for three days in a row, she would be off. It wouldn't take long for her to catch up to Alphy and Fatal, but...

"This sucks. I can't believe I had to work through the first few days of game launch," she grumbled to herself. Wrapped in huge, fluffy cotton towels, she poked through her closet, looking for just the right outfit for work—blue work shirt or red? "Hmm," she said. "Today is a red day." After pulling on the plain, anonymous uniform, khaki pants and red collared shirt, she crimped her drying hair. She paused, noticing something out of place. Her nostrils flared; she could smell coffee wafting in the air, but didn't remember starting the pot.

Quietly, she took the few steps to the doorway and glanced into the small kitchenette to find two women—red hair and pink hair—and one man, way too young for all that white hair to be natural, sitting at her table. All dressed in black suits with white shirts and black ties; each had a to-go cup filled with coffee, and there, in front of the empty chair that she always sat in, was a fourth to-go cup.

Stunned, so much so that she didn't make a peep, Janus inspected each set of eyes staring back at her. "Good morning, Miss Panikar. My name is Margaret," the redhead said, touching her chest above her heart with fingers, then pointing to the woman next to her. "This little beauty is Sara." Pink nodded at Janus, then Red reached across the small table and patted Whitey on the arm. "And this little hotty is Lenny. We picked him up yesterday." Red had hungry eyes for her two companions, then turned them to Janus with a small grin. The other two at the table lifted their coffee cups in a salute and said, "Good morning, Miss Panikar," as if they were in grade school addressing a teacher, then they sipped.

"Why are you in my apartment? I don't have any money in the house. It's all on plastic. You can—"

"Miss Panikar, we aren't here to take anything or to assault you in any way." Margaret interrupted. "We would like to discuss a job opportunity with you. Something more rewarding and challenging than working the register at the electronics warehouse. Starting today."

Janus was baffled at the situation, and asked, "Okay, so why would you break into my home for a job interview?"

Margaret smiled a little broader, her massive canines peeping out just a little bit, eyes narrowing as she bashfully fluttered her very long red lashes. She always loved this part, when they had enough courage to ask the obvious things.

Well, eventually Margaret would tell her, but Janus was cute, and she wanted to play with her for a little while first, then give her the meaty details. Margaret explained, "You have been picked, along with several others, based on surveillance analysis over the last year."

Margaret paused and slowly stood up. "Janus, we can take a walk outside or go to a library or some other public place if you would be more comfortable." It always helped to give them options. Options made them feel like they had control, and that was when they were really vulnerable.

Janus picked up her coffee and sniffed it. "Surveillance? Me? Is this a caramel latte?"

Margaret smiled again. "Why, yes, it is. We know how much you like them... with coconut creamer." She flashed Sara a knowing grin that was returned. "Now, stay here to talk, or go somewhere else?"

Janus reasoned to herself that they hadn't touched her or tried to threaten her, and her anxiety eased a little. "Hmm." She pondered then took a sip, eyeing Margaret. Margaret was acting like one of the supervisors at the electronics warehouse when they trained new employees. She had that air of enjoying her control. Janus stretched her hand out in a welcoming gesture to the living room. Light was flooding in through a large opened window onto the big, comfortable couch in there. "Please," Janus said, "bring your trainees onto the couch so we can get comfortable. I am sure you have much to talk about." Lenny and Sara looked at each other then at Margaret, blushing slightly.

Margaret's eyes widened and she let out a little laugh. "I knew you were a good pick for this, Janus."

Margaret and Sara pounced on the couch, pinning Lenny between them, with a familiarity for each other that corporate America couldn't tolerate in the current PC environment. They were very casual and intrusive with each other's personal space; though Lenny looked a bit awkward and flustered, seemed comfortable with the arrangement.

They had just picked Lenny up yesterday, Margaret explained, so he must have been in Janus's position. Janus couldn't help feeling excited about the threesome lounging on the coach before her. She flopped down in her big reading chair. The sun angled over her shoulder and warmed the uninvited guests. "So, tell me everything, especially why I am under surveillance, and make it snappy. I won't be late to work."

Left eyebrow arching, Margaret smiled again. Janus was going to be a real pleasure to work with. "Well," Margaret began, "for starters, when you agreed to the EULA and the other license agreements for the beta version of Total Quest, you opted into the selective service volunteer program operated through Total VR and their affiliates. This is how we have been legally monitoring you since you started the beta testing. We are one of the affiliated corporations that own a very large piece of Total VR."

Janus scrunched her brows together. She was ready for life to change again. Total Quest Beta was amazing. It had helped her discover something inside of herself: a leader, a warrior, a hunger to conquer and plunder. The physical demands of the game had put her in good health. She even jogged now, a couple of miles every day, putting her in the prime of her game, her life. However, she still had one foot in her old life, stuck in the mundane, no options, the past beginning to repeat. Before the game, she was meek and submissive, with a bad habit of doing whatever people said. But now, she commanded, but with only one foot, one foot in the excitement, one foot in a virtual world bent on adventure. Work was money to play that game. The electronics warehouse had been like living out a life sentence, like living back home, chained and locked at a cash register, chained without hope of parole, no hope, just the escape into the beta.

"If your company owns Total VR, what do they want with me and why did you break in?" Janus asked.

Margaret connected eyes with Janus and let her smile fade just a touch. "First, call me Mar, Janus. You are a great leader and skilled warrior. Your leadership performance, matched up with your battle skills, has piqued our interest. We would like to offer you a position in our militarized program. We form squads in game and train in the virtual setting. Basically, we are mercenaries, mercs in Total Quest. Twelve squads compete in game, the top three squads move on to a new playing field and matches. The top squad of the twelve not only gets to progress, but receives a massive cash bonus and gear upgrades. Sound fun? Get paid to play the game?"

A loud purring resonated from the couch as Mar mindlessly scratched Sara on the top of the head. Sara seemed like she was about to fall asleep with the sun baking and the scalp scratch. Smashing up against a flushed Lenny to reach Sara, Margaret stretched her already broad smile, this time letting her massive canines catch the sun coming in from the opened window behind Janus. She knew it was very alluring and dramatic. She waited for Janus to respond. She would. Mar knew Janus well. Her interviewees always broke the silence first. This wasn't her first time around recruiting for Griffith, but it was the most fun she'd had doing it. She snuggled closer to a grinning Lenny, laying her head on his shoulder and gently petting Sara. Sara's eyes were glossy slits. It looked like she was asleep, purring like a motor now. All three enjoyed the comfort of the big couch and the warmth of the sun on black suits. Lenny was a great score, catching on pretty quick. They would get Thai food after this, then maybe find some local bands to check out in the evening. Definitely dancing, they had to go dancing. Having Sara as her second was a real blessing from Mother Wep, blessed mother of all. And Lenny! The hot little newbie, mmm. Mar couldn't wait to go dancing with all three of them. Janus was dead sexy, and always fun to watch. Mar heated up thinking about the night ahead of them. Wep, she loved her job.

Margaret had stopped talking, as Janus politely sipped her coffee, her delicious caramel coffee, and casually eyed the three strangers on the couch. The direct sun on the couch was meant to pressure them, but they seemed at complete ease, reclined in odd positions. They looked like teenagers at a friend's house, on Janus's couch, as if they were old friends. Maybe they thought she *was* an old friend. They had been monitoring her activities for over a year, at least the red-haired woman had. Oh, what big teeth she had. So, Margaret probably felt incredibly comfortable, already in a familiar environment from monitoring Janus's apartment. That meant they had been in her apartment before, maybe to investigate her belongings for information the game activities wouldn't have given... like her favorite coffee drink. Observing each one, noting how satisfied they looked, Janus found herself longing to join them, to blend in with them. She wanted to ditch the red shirt and khaki pants for a black suit.

Janus was in sharp contrast to them, khaki slacks and red collared sport shirt, with the store logo stitched over the heart. Everything about them looked exciting and fresh: their hair, Margaret a deep red in contrast to her blue eyes and milk-white skin, Sara's light pink pixie cut, soft white skin, and slanted green eyes, and even Lenny looked exciting, with shaggy white hair and a reddish sunburn look to his skin, and his eyes were glinting excitement. Janus was mundane, average, easily passing as an Indian or Pakistani girl, or sometimes Mexican or even African, she had light brown skin, caramel-brown hair, and brown eyes. Mundane, at least in appearance. She knew she had more to offer. She wanted more. They were dressed in stylish black suits and were extremely well manicured.

Janus took a deep breath and let it out slowly. Margaret's smile slipped a bit when she did this. Anything Margret offered in job form, freakishly large canines or not, Janus knew she was going to say yes. Already, she'd figured out why they broke into her apartment. It was a display of power. Showing her they could. This company simply did whatever it wanted, and now, it wanted her. Paid gaming. If she played it right, she would be in a black suit doing what she wanted, or at least not chained to a cash register. She sipped on her coffee, still waiting for Margaret to finish, not wanting to be rude. Margaret's pleasant smile had faded to a dreamy grin, and beads of perspiration formed on her forehead as she stared anxiously at Janus. Father had taught Janus not to finish the thoughts of others, because that would lead to wrong assumptions. That would lead into poor decision making. So she waited patiently for Margaret, her white cheeks flushing a brilliant red. Janus would call work after this conversation. Today she could be late. Listening to the job offer was so exciting, but she was ethical; she would have to give appropriate two-week notice, as that was the right thing to do, but yes, she could be late.

5: 4 OF 12 OF 12

After Janus accepted the offer from Mar and unintentionally won the silence contest, Mar insisted that Janus celebrate with them for the rest of the day. Mar was her new boss, after all, so demanded that Janus call the warehouse to tell them she was not coming in. They had important things to discuss and do, Mar told her. "After all, Jan," she said, "you are giving them two weeks as of today. They can survive one day without you. We need to celebrate!"

Janus wanted to do it. Mar was just the excuse she needed, they both knew it, and laughed together as Janus made the call to work.

"This is Janus Panikar," she said into the phone after a familiar coworker greeted her. "Oh hi, Smitty! How are you?" She listened attentively. "Oh, no, sounds terribly busy. Hey, tell Mark I'm not coming in today. Mental reasons. Also tell him to check his email for my two weeks' notice, okay? Thanks, Smitty, bye." It was done. She was free. Almost. Still two weeks left.

Mar, Sara, and Lenny all cheered. "Okay, let's eat! Where do you want to go, Jan-Jan?" Margaret said, canines glistening with a grin.

"Oh, I don't go out to eat. I can cook something here..."

"No!" Sara said. "We want to go out, Jan-Jan!"

Janus thought a moment as she tapped her cheek, then suggested, "How about a sandwich shop? I haven't tried a sub yet."

"No! We need something fancy, Janus!" Mar demanded as she stamped her foot. "The Thai Place!"

At the restaurant, before the boba tea on the river walk, Jan had signed the contract and stuck her finger into a box. The small box captured her fingerprint and gently pricked her for a blood sample. "It's to build your access keys and bind you to the company," Mar explained. "Just don't tell anyone outside the company about anything you do or experience, and that includes us. You are now on the Griffith payroll." Margaret winked and licked her right fang.

Lenny cut in, "I just did it yesterday, Janus— " and Sara blurted, "Never do this again for anyone else, Jan-Jan! You really shouldn't let us do it either, but we actually have a great setup for you. Griffith is huge and usually gets first dibs in most of the trade. They are one of the largest corporations in the galaxy! Anywhere you go you have the benefits and privileges that go along with being employed by Griffith. You're really gonna love it. Especially the travel." Janus smiled in excitement as Sara asked with a devilish grin, "As a new Griffith employee, what secrets would you like to know first?"

"How do I get a suit like that?" She was still in her khakis and red shirt.

Lenny laughed. "That was the first thing I asked, remember?" He nudged Margaret in the ribs.

Margaret narrowed her eyes at Janus and said, "Jan, you really are ready for a change, aren't you? I told Central you were ready." Margaret's eyes softened. "Every day at the warehouse, I could see you wasting away just a little bit more, day by day, outgrowing your environment, your peers. We could have snagged you months ago." She scratched Lenny behind the ears, then, with her other hand, stroked Sara's soft pink hair, still looking at Janus. "I'm glad I got dibs on you. I know how strong you are. And I like you already."

Janus flushed. "Oh, well..." she mumbled, and Lenny said, "Damn, Mar, you just scared the shit out of her." He leaned over and patted Janus on the arm. "She is very affectionate, but also very respectful of boundaries. She is referring to her raiding team, her squad. We're building to twelve."

"Of course," Janus said, nodding. "I understand. This is all so unbelievable and perfect..."

Mar burst out laughing and said "To the riverfront! Boba, then suits!"

They walked and window-shopped, sipping on their boba tea. Janus hadn't tried it before, so Margaret had insisted. "You will have taro; it's my favorite, with the large boba bubbles—they're extra chewy!"

They were in and out of clothiers and fashion stores, but it was at the tailor Friedman Daniels that Margaret stopped the party. "You are gonna love it here." She opened the door for the troop to enter. Lenny and Sara both made enthusiastic sounds of agreement. They all walked in, and a man and woman dressed in tweed and leather-patched jackets welcomed them.

"Margi!" they exclaimed. "Ready for a fitting?" the man asked. The woman said, "Are you going to let me free your tail? It's so lovely and would accent the new black silk florakin bolt we just received."

Janus gasped in embarrassment yet again, so crass these people were, her new crew. And these tailors trying to show off Mar's behind, to boot. Margaret exclaimed, "No tail!" as she slapped her hands on her buttocks. "I haven't been given approval to show off my tail. It's not like anyone would think it's real anyways, with all the crazy cosplayers now."

The man nodded in agreement and sympathetically said, "Yes, yes. It is such a shame, but you should let us cut one for you, so it is ready when you are. Yes?"

"You know," Sara said, "that's a splendid idea. I will do that, let you fit me, if you can convince Margaret to do it. Anyways, I don't want another lovely power suit. I want something for the night, when I hunt. Something for the clubs."

Margaret growled. "Look, I think it's a great idea, but they said I was on a leash now."

Sara stroked Mar's hair. "What is she going to do? Tell you to leave and go back?" At that, they both laughed loud and hard. Margaret thumbed her left fang's point and slowly turned to Janus, then she slid off her black jacket, letting it fall to the ground.

The woman gasped and said, "Quick, Ray, grab your tape and chalk!" Mar began loosening her tie, and Sara dropped her jacket too. Mar, still watching Janus as if she were doing something crazy, smiled and said, "Janus." She snapped her tie off her neck like a whip. "Tell me, Janus, do you think it's a good idea?"

She undid a few buttons then pulled her shirt over her head and tossed it to Lenny, who was trying to hold back his laughter while keeping an eye on Janus. Janus looked at Sara, Lenny, and Margaret, wondering why they were staring at her. Mar and Sara were taking their clothes off in front of everyone, not her. What the hell were they doing? In a moment, the two new female workmates were standing in front of Janus in their skivvies, laughing as if the joke was on her. Lenny had gathered the garments into a bundled wad in his arms. Ray said, "Here, Lenny, give those to me. I'll freshen them up so they don't get wrinkles. Kim will start the measurements. She's been waiting to cut these for months."

Janus looked at Kim, who squealed. "Both of you? I get to make new ones for both of you? To show off your tails?" Lenny burst out laughing, causing Sara and Margaret to start up again too. Lenny pointed to Janus. "The look on your face... Girls, just turn around already—" but before he could finish, Janus saw the swishing of pink and dark red behind the women.

Holding her hands to her face, she gasped. "Oh my God, you have tails! Not your butts, tails. They look so real. I thought she meant your behinds."

All four of them broke into laughter, until Kim said, "But they are, dear. They are real."

Margaret reached up and fingered her hair for a moment, pulling away several very large bobby pins, releasing two large, fluffy, pointed ears. Wide-eyed, Janus turned to Sara just in time to see a set of smaller pink ears spring up from her hair. Sara and Margaret, both with the toothiest grins Janus had ever seen, stood snickering and giggling like little kids.

"Just like the games. You have costumes from cos-play from games?" Janus said.

Lenny roared with laughter. Margaret patted Kim on the shoulder and pointed to Janus. "She needs a work suit, ASAP. I want something green and sexy for my tail—nightclub shit. Sara was right about that. No work suit, but I will look at the florakin silk. It feels amazing." Sara chimed in, "Same, but I'll let you pick my colors, Kim. No work suits today."

Janus watched their swishing tails and twitching ears, then mumbled, "You're both beastkin. Oh, wow. You're both beastkin..."

She looked to Lenny, who held up his hands. "Mundane human, just like you."

Janus stood dumbfounded as Kim called to her partner, "Ray, three fittings, get Denny from the back." She turned to Janus and said, "How about a party outfit for you too, dear?"

Janus didn't answer, so Sara did for her. "Well, of course, Kim, that is a wonderful idea."

Margaret began to laugh again, recounting the last few minutes with great delight, and the raid team started a fresh round of laughter. Janus joined in this time.

Wearing a black power suit of florakin silk, Janus stepped out of the fitting room, blending right in with her new crew. The silk was amazing. Thick, so thick, but it felt as if she weren't wearing it at all, and oh, how soft it was. She didn't know if she would be able to wear anything else ever again. Sara reassured her, "Don't worry, Jan-Jan, the skirt and top will feel just as good. You should go back for some nighties. Those are divine."

They finished up and Margaret put it all on her tab.

"It's your uniform Jan Jan. It's my job to keep you all looking classy and hot! Now let's go dancing!"

"Well, I would really like to kill some stuff for a few hours first. Would that be okay?" Janus asked.

"We could log on tonight for a few hours." Lenny said. " We can launch our big Trinity reunion party at the starting lens. I'll call Alphy for you. You know his real name is Alfredo, Alfredo Margo Lopez?"

At that, Janus's jaw dropped "Wait, you're Fatal? I thought you lived on the West Coast. What are you doing here?"

"I'm here to sweeten the deal, in case you had said no." Lenny answered. "They recruited me after we took down the king. They were there with us fighting. On the beach, I said yes before the beta went black. I spent last night getting fitted, wined, and dined, too." He laughed. "We flew in before Friedman's closed, it was my first stop. Anyways, I can text Alpha Beta that we are go for tonight if you want?"

Margaret chimed in, "Great idea! I wanted to go dancing tonight anyways. This is perfect. We can have beastkin music and those sexy florakin."

"Oh please," Sara said. "Florakin are easy. I like the humans; they are far more fun to play with than florakin. Just look at Janus. She's changing color even now!"

Janus was blushing again.

Margaret got a little serious. "When you log on, my call name is Cherry Bomb, Sara is Pinky, and you know Lenny is Fatal. You, Panic, are 4.12.12. Fourth teammate of the twelfth squad of the twelve squads. I'm 1.12.12—got it?" As Janus nodded, Sara added, "Griffith will be recruiting a total of 120 players, including you and Lenny, that perform above standards. Twelve squads of twelve, all with veteran mercs and their seconds like Mar and me, to train up the new players for combat readiness and the big competition."

"Our squad got the short end of the deal," Mar interjected.

"We have to let the other squads fill in before we do. We're last pick on the rotation. But somehow Mar convinced central command at Griffith to let us have two of the top three Betas," Sara explained. "She was pushing for all three of you, since we're on the end, but Kiri's eleventh squad got whoever we didn't take."

Mar said, "We picked Lenny and you. Too hot to pass."

Sara continued, "The other firsts and seconds don't like us that much, Mar and me. We have a history, a different view than they do on just about everything." At this, Margaret and Sara locked eyes with knowing smiles, erupting in laughter then giggles.

Margaret continued, "It is part of your job description, in addition to your personal training, to train up other players in your class. Then recommend them to Sara or me, if they are a possible fit. We can check them out and see if they are a good match for the program, then present them to the selective service recruitment list. If the other squads pass on them, they are ours."

Janus said, "That hardly sounds fair. If we find good teammates, shouldn't we get them?"

Sara answered, "That's what Mar said to central command, and that's how we have the two of you. I'm second to Mar, and we have plenty of experience to share with you. I think we will have the strongest squad regardless of the trash we end up with. Who knows, maybe we'll get lucky."

6: BORIS ARROW

Preordered with launch-day delivery option, Boris received the Total VR deluxe package at six in the morning, on schedule for the release and launch of the new world version of Total Quest. The game had been live since 00:01 this morning. That was military time, a very useful way of dividing the day into its twenty-four hours, avoiding any miscommunication errors that could be made with the popular twelve-hour competing system. The game had been live, but the gear to play it, unless you were a beta, had not been available to the public until this moment—for him, 06:00. Perhaps he should adjust to a twenty-four-hour UTC time standard. This was worldwide, after all. The twenty-four-hour system only worked for its time zone. So that would make it 06:00-08:00. Or at least his relative sunlight was -8. UTC time was now 14:00. This was a rabbit trail for later.

A self-made entrepreneur, he was master of his destiny and his surroundings. The only distractions he had to take care of when he wanted his playtime were wife and kids. The first few weeks of the game would be like the great land rush. Whoever got there first and had the strength to keep it won the long race, establishing the in-game political structure. This game had it all: quests and missions, hand-to-hand combat, land management and settlement building, crafting and merchandising—everything, all in one. He was going to be the Emperor of Total Quest. He just needed a couple weeks to establish himself, stake his claim. Ken would do the rest.

Boris had booked the family a two-week vacation in Florida. The wife and kids always loved going to Disney World with plenty of spending cash. No distractions. Pure game time.

He set the freshly delivered package down next to his provisions box and then sat on the ground next to it. Carefully, he dissected the contents of the package, gingerly placing each piece in the box into its designated place on the ground before him: one full sensory playpen, one game codex, one motion-sensor suit, one console, one console power cord, one backup data power cord to connect console and helmet, and one special edition black skull helmet with flip goggle. The "special" part of "special edition" gave his in-game avatar the option of wearing the black skull helmet graphic over any other gear he might have on. Now he opened the provisions box: one catheter pre-lubed with antimicrobial ointment and collection bladder, one hydration tube, one hydration flask and backpack, one nutrition-bar dispenser—ten-bar capacity—one case of 144 nutrition bars. He grabbed one of the bars and sank his teeth into it, holding it like a cigar. Flavorless. The game would enhance it with whatever in-game meal he ate. It was firm from the cool temperature but would soften with chewing, and would fill a player up for hours. Eating in the game added extra boons to the players' characters, different boons for different meals. With the bar hanging out of his mouth, he picked up the game codex and stood up.

Walking over to the large east-facing window overlooking the backyard garden, he plopped into his oversized leather chair. He glanced around the game room and grinned, readying himself for the early morning codex study. *Knowledge is power.* The sun was rising in front of him. He always sat facing east in the morning, soaking in the early light, a new day for a new world. He opened the codex, noted his unique initialization code, and began to read.

7: KENNETH ARROW

> *"Value is as valuable as we make it. Some people spend thousands of dollars to eat the briny eggs of fish, to feel the tiny little balls burst in their mouth, all salty and slick." Jan Jan*

Ken was doing the pee-pee dance waiting in the checkout line. Since he was a kid, he had learned that doing physical activity when the bladder was full was the best way to hold it. Half a liter of coffee was pressing on his bladder now. At six a.m., the store had opened early for the launch of Total Quest. The first customer in the door was Ken. Double-checking his wallet again for his preorder voucher for the

Total VR deluxe edition gaming package, he confirmed it was there, for the third time in the last hour. When he walked through the doors, pyramids of the boxed game sets stretched out in front of him in the middle of the regular aisles. He plucked one from the nearest stack, size medium, and tucked the large box under his arm. The VR gear was needed to play Total Quest, a full sensory immersion virtual reality game. With over a year of beta testers working out all the kinks and mechanics, today was the release and launch of the game and gear to the public. With game gear secured, Ken wandered the aisles in awe of all the electronics displayed. This place was a warehouse of anything and everything a gamer or technical guru would love: cables, plugs, routers, televisions, antennae, everything. Moving from row to row, Ken froze in front of a 250-centimeter curved ultra-high-definition television. Lilo. She was jumping off a building, falling through the traffic of flying cars to crash through the top of Cory's taxi. Ah, *The Seven Elements*, definitely in Ken's top ten all-time favorite movies.

"Nice, isn't it?"

"Oh, man. Yeah, it's amazing," Ken responded.

"It's yours for about $250 a month—not bad, right?"

Ken turned to see the eager eyes of the salesman sizing him up. Without a word in response, Ken tucked his head and walked away to the checkout line.

He had spent too much time watching the movie instead of getting in line to make the shopping visit a quick in-and-out. Ken found himself at the end of a huge, quickly growing line of gamers with gear, tech masters with co-ax cables and crimpers, and all the other types of electronics customers in between, all grumbling about the time wasted in the massive line. He took his place, and time itself seemed to slow down. At least he could still see *The Seven Elements* playing in the television department. "Gwar thwack!" his stomach growled. Resisting the urge to compulsively snack on all the food items and drinks along the way, Ken turned his head from the chilled Mountain Dew, the Jack's beef jerky, and the Flamin' Hot Cheetos. All of these temptations and snacks were conveniently displayed within arm's reach of the captive consumers. Every penny would be needed for the Total VR deluxe edition gaming console. Ken's preorder voucher ensured he would leave with one, and had only been a hundred-dollar dent of a deposit; the rest of the high-priced item would be taken out of his shallow pockets.

Enduring the first thirty minutes in line, fighting the compulsive desire to rip into some tasty snacks, Ken was feeling pretty good about himself. That was right before his bladder pressure fell into the red zone. Out of nowhere, a bolt in the blue zapped his pee bag. Pee-pee dance time. Tensely he struggled for fifteen minutes, barely moving a muscle or his place in line. Now he began to gasp and moan from the pain, and the wriggles set in. The others in line around him began to lose tolerance for his squirming and gasping. Many of those minutes he had questioned himself if the gaming console was worth the pain of a bladder stretched beyond repair. But, finding his resolution, Ken loudly blurted, "Yes, It's worth it!" The man in front of him looked back with startled eyes and then walked to register six. Ken hadn't noticed the line had moved so far forward. Finally, he was next. Wriggling—his bladder felt like it had a tiny rupture—but he couldn't leave the line now. It was a mega line trailing behind him; he wouldn't start all over. The Total VR gear and game would soon be his, then he could pee.

A female voice, already overused and gentle, straining to be adequately cheerful, according to store policy, beckoned to Ken. "Sir, I can help you at register three." Squeezing his thighs as hard as he could—the coffee was going to win soon—he shuffled his feet, legs locked at the knees, to register three. She was cute, so he tried to play it cool and stared at her nametag: *Team member Janus.* Sweating profusely, doubled over in pain and wide-eyed, he turned his face up, smiling at her. She recoiled slightly as a droplet of sweat fell from the tip of his nose, puddling on her counter. As she scanned the gaming console, Ken slid his credit card and the preorder voucher toward her. His body was shaking, face turning red; he was unsure if he would stay dry through the transaction.

She reached out hesitantly, picked the card up, and swiped it while forcing an adequate smile. The machine beeped a stressful alarm. "Sir," Janus began as she slid the card back to Ken with one finger, "your credit card doesn't cover all of it." She dispensed some hand sanitizer from the bottle next to her and rubbed briskly. "You still owe $1009.63." Ken did a standing crunch with his abs, then let out a primal "Ha!" He could hold it. Janus jumped again, eyes wide with surprise, and glanced over at the security guard by the front door. The only things more alarming than the security guard's yellow shirt were her deadly eyes drilling a hole through Ken's face. Twitching and gasping, with the greatest care not to make any weird movements, Ken used one finger to gingerly slide his debit card to Janus. Her face flushed red against a light tan while her sparkling brown eyes narrowed. Ken performed little bounces on the balls of his feet. It was helping. The debit card slid through the register, pulling every last penny out of his bank account. There was a small transition in Janus's face—it was pity. "Oh, sir. You still owe $7.63." This she said so gently and full of empathy that you would have thought he had just lost a favorite pet. Bladder screaming for release, Ken bent down, touching his toes then shot his feet out behind into push-up position.

The yellow shirt popped up and briskly walked over to join Janus at register three. She whispered loud enough for everyone to hear, "Janus, is everything okay?" Janus peered down at Ken and mumbled, "I have no idea." After he ground out two strenuous push-ups, arms shaking and stomach convulsing the whole time, his throat let out an "ugh." It worked: the dam held back the flood. Good ole exercise. Then something new hit Ken: reality. He popped up like a deranged human jack-in-the-box, his face twisted in pain. "Ah, crap..." Unconsciously wiping his brow, he muttered to himself then patted his pockets, all of them, even shirt pockets. Though the urgency to urinate had temporarily subsided, good sense washed freely through his brain, as he realized he had just gone deeper into debt and cleared out his bank account for a video game. He could feel his face drooping, and looked at Janus, then yellow shirt and her piercing eyes, then at the register. Janus brought her cuffed fingers to her lips. She cleared her throat and said, "The game... Total Quest... It's amazing. I play a warrior. The sensory immersion is better than reality, and it's physically intense. I played beta the full year. I only work to play Total Quest now. Ha." Her eyes unlocked from Ken's and trailed back to the register. That sealed the deal.

Reaching as deep as he could into his front-right pants pocket, Ken grasped the paper key, the green note, a monetary solution to all the lonely nights and weekends in store for him. Ken could live on peanut butter and water for a month. As he slammed his last ten dollars in a single bill on the counter, the security guard jumped, her hand hovering over her Taser like a gunslinger in *The Good, the Bad and the Ugly*. "Here," Ken said, moving away from the register, doing the shuffle, "put the change in my bag and leave it with your yellow bodyguard. I'll be back. I have to use the toilet."

8: INTRODUCTIONS

Back at his apartment, Ken set the gear on the countertop. Finally, the new Total VR system, tried and tested, ranked as the top VR immersion gear, and a proprietary match for its newly released game, Total Quest, was his. An extreme lightweight helmet came in a variety of colors and styles. In his haste grabbing the box, Ken had picked out a dark blue helmet with a red and black racing stripe running down the middle, from brow to nape. It came equipped with a built-in sound system that cupped your ears with marshmallow foam to totally block out real-world noise. When set up, the playpen surrounded the player with sensors and nodes, linking game activities and player movements for an amazing, full sensory immersive experience. Utilizing vibration nodes all over the helmet and body suit, it was supposed to give realistic sensory experience in all kinds of situations. The goggle-like visor could flip down and seal with a wide radius around the eyes, providing an infinite peripheral view of ultra-realistic virtual imagery. Yes. Giddy as a freshman dating the homecoming queen, Ken squeezed the garment bag until the package bubbled and popped. The smell of clinically sterile poly-spandex blend poofed from the vacuum-sealed pouch containing the black motion-sensor jumper. Ken whipped it out like a matador, then pulled it close to himself, sizing it up to his body. Putting on the machine-washable, full-length, finger-to-toe body gear was quick and easy. The jumper had a thick, hearty plastic zipper from the crotch all the way up to the front collar, with nerve clusters all over the suit pressing gently into his skin. The nerve clusters did everything from vibrate to change temperature. Standing up, Ken performed large windmills with his arms then kicked his legs around like a crazy chicken to snug the fit. The suit fell into place.

He picked up the codex and set it on a small table next to a sealed bottle of whiskey with six months of dust built up on it. There it would stay. From the crash course he had taken with his brother Boris, Ken knew that "players should wear the total body system until complete initialization has been confirmed by the player's artificial gaming intelligence liaison." The AGI player liaison was the link between the player and the game. Player liaisons were responsible for unique scripting—scripting was the term used to describe the computer language written into the game software to create NPCs, monsters, environment, and quests—for the player. Ken was ready to initialize. Breakfast could wait. After donning the helmet and flipping the goggles down, Ken reached back to press the power button located on the nape of the headpiece, and it connected wirelessly to the console. The goggle lenses, default clear, powered up and darkened to a total blackout, then again faded clear as the system powered up.

The helmet came pre-charged with forty-eight hours of playtime. Built into the helmet, the batteries only took thirty minutes to fully recharge. Technically players could stay in game while still plugged in to recharge or have a hard data connection, but that was not encouraged due to possible entanglement and strangulation. His vision cleared except for a blinking, thin-lined red bull's-eye—the bull's-eye had crosshairs and looked like the reticle on a first-person shooter game, and seemed to be just out of focus. Ken took a deep breath. Concentrating on the red reticle, he moved his vision's depth around until the reticle came into focus an arm's length away. His suit came alive at the same time the reticle came into focus. He could feel it constricting and vibrating all over his body, sending chills and tingles all over. The reticle turned from red to blue, and the system sounded a faint chirp, like a distant smoke detector running low on batteries. A female voice softly greeted him. "Hello, thank you for using Total VR systems. Please read the EULA and legally binding contract information. You may agree by saying 'yes' or disagree by saying 'no' ..."

"Yes," Ken blurted out, voice heavy with anticipation.

"Do you understand that, by using this software and hardware, you lawfully consent to the Total VR corporation and all of its affiliates? Say—"

"Yes," Ken blurted with even more excitement.

"To begin initialization, you must enter the—"

"Yes, please," Ken interrupted. "Please begin initialization." Heart racing, he could barely control himself. The first pangs of discovery were still pulsing through his body. This was a smart thing he was talking to, like a person! It was an intelligence after all, even if it was artificially made, just for gaming. The system chirped several more times, paused, then his suit pulsed with slight temperature flux and random sensations. Nothing extreme, just light pokes and brushings, like a cat walking past your shins. He could feel a breeze then a raindrop as a distant range of noises passed from his left over his head to the right. Oh, wow, this was cool. Registration was next on the list. Filling out his registration information seemed pretty standard: name, address, phone number, service provider, and all his contact information—even the bank account information that the now-empty debit card belonged to, for future quick in-game purchases. That would be a while. Ken was ready for the next step. "Name your player," it stated.

Breath stuck in his throat. This was a moment he had been anticipating. He was sure his first choice for a gamertag, the name his avatar would be called, would already be taken by one of the beta players. But he was still going to give it a try. A gamertag was a way to relate to yourself by third person, allowing you to completely separate yourself in suspended disbelief. Two people, you and your avatar, who was actually you. Call yourself by a different name, and all actions and decisions were owned by your gamertag, not really you. You entered not just the game but your character. For just a moment, Ken second-guessed his pick, remembering all of his favorite fictional heroes "Uh," Ken stammered, feeling the pressure of finality. Squeezing his eyes shut, desperate to get into the game with his preferred tag—Ken would love and cherish it for all eternity—that spark of hope brightened in his mind. "Okay, I think I'm ready to name my avatar." Then Ken sheepishly stated the name as a question: "Kar?" Kar was the ultimate hero of all time. The warrior in the manga *Killer Warrior*, Kar was legendary for his sword-hacking skills. "Hello, Kar," the AGI responded in her light female voice. Wide-eyed, Ken mumbled, "Astounding. It's mine..." A wide grin stretched over his face. This was starting off fantastically.

The AGI continued, "As your artificial gaming intelligence player liaison, what would you like to call me?"

"What? What do you mean?"

"What would you like to call me when you address me?"

Surprised by the question, Ken asked, "You don't have a name?"

"No, not until you give me one. It is not necessary to name me; I am preset to respond to 'AGI,' 'computer,' 'player liaison,' or 'liaison.' It is not a strictly defined variable unless you decide on a specific name."

"Ah." *Why not go all the way with it?* Ken thought. "Your name, it's gonna be... Vera," Ken said with great enthusiasm, making up for the sheepish "Kar?" In *Killer Warrior*, Vera was the love interest Kar dedicated himself to. Not that Ken was going to dedicate himself to this AGI, but the nostalgia was simply irresistible.

"Are you satisfied with the current voice settings for Vera, or would you like to access settings to change Vera's voice attributes?" Vera inquired.

"Hmm." Ken greatly enjoyed customization options, so responded, "Access voice attributes." The visor remained clear, but a list of voice attribute categories was displayed in black text against the background of his barren studio wall. The blue target followed his eye movement, opening each category that he looked at into dropdown menu selections.

"Ken, you have opened all of the options and sub-options. I do not think you have read the codex. Is this true?" Vera asked.

"I can read it later," Ken responded.

"It is in my protocol to inform you it is dangerous to skip codex. On average, it takes four hours to read it thoroughly. Outside of my protocol, I would tell you, Ken, that the codex is not necessary. We can complete initialization without the codex. I will walk you through proper procedures as we encounter them as I have done thus far. However, my protocols forbid me to give this option to you unless you specifically ask to skip codex initialization. Is that agreeable to you, Ken?"

Ken remembered the crash course warning against not using the instructions in the codex, but he had already gotten this far without it. So what if a few nuts and bolts were left over? Figuring things out on his own terms was part of the joy of discovering new things. Ken took a deep breath and responded, "Sure, Vera. That actually sounds like a great idea." He cleared his throat and said in a monotone formal manner, "I specifically want to skip codex initialization." He smiled—he liked being in charge—and continued, "You can guide me through the process. Do you have any other suggestions—or, I mean, if you have things you can't tell me, can you tell me what you can't? I guess just please let me know."

Vera made a light chirp—or, at least, he thought it was her doing that. Did she understand what he'd said? She responded, "Codex standard initialization has been removed. Hard initialization has been initiated. I have reset the voice attributes page for you." Sure enough, the view before him was clear again; all the dialogues he had inadvertently opened were cleaned up. "Wow, that's better. Thanks, Vera."

"You're welcome, Ken. As you read through options, do not look directly at the text. Try to read the text while your eyes are focused on the spaces above or below the text. When you see an option that you want to access, look directly at it. Together, we can calibrate it to respond in a comfortable amount of time, according to your desires."

"Okay," Ken said as he looked directly at the voice attributes text. A sub-list opened up beneath the first line of text to display three choices. From top to bottom: androgynous, female, male.

"Hmm." Ken tapped his chin. Was this AGI he'd named Vera a man or woman or neither? "Are you male or female?" The system seemed to lag for a response. Maybe only a few seconds, but for the console and its processing power, that seemed a very long time to answer a simple question. Vera said in her default soothing female voice, "I am an AGI, artificial gaming intelligence, a sapient entity created without specific gender. It is not a strictly defined variable. I can reproduce without sexual organs; there is no sexual reproduction pathway. I do not possess male or female anatomy to suggest either, for lack of a physical form."

Wow, he thought, that was a very well-answered response for game software. "Okay," Ken started, "reset voice attributes to your preferences, Vera." Again, the faint chirping sound, this time a full twenty seconds passing before Vera responded. Ken was going to check his network connection to see if it was causing the slow response time. Then, an ominous, deep, booming voice resounded low and softly, and his whole body felt it wash over, as if a large wave had engulfed him. "Voice attributes reset to my specifications." Ken's jaw dropped, adrenaline flushed his system, and his eyebrows arched in humor and amazement.

9: BREAKFAST

"Start every day with butter coffee and heavy cream along with a fat- and protein-rich meal, like bacon!" Duck n Frog Café

The rest of the initializing was, admittedly, a bit mundane. Vera had instructed Ken to go about regular activities, while talking to her, narrating, or, more accurately, acting as his own color commentator. Vera ate up every action and word Ken gave her. Often, she would make him repeat a word or body movement. Being the center of an individual's focus, other than his blessed mother, was a unique experience for Ken. He had never been successful in the dating scene. The only friend that had lasted more than a week or two after discovering his quirkiness was his older brother, but he was eight years older than Ken and treated him like a little kid.

"Vera, this is really cool. I feel like I'm at a party, the way you keep changing your voice." Ken was in lonely guy heaven. Vera continued to entertain him with her demands, switching up the voice settings with each new barrage of questions. In a commanding voice like the actor who played a sky city mayor in a space opera, she demanded, "Repeat the word you just used!" then later, as frog puppet, "Explain why you are flossing after you brush your teeth." Then, as he visited the toilet, an old, scratchy, androgynous voice: "How often do you urinate in an eight-hour period?" In a youthful tone she stumped him by saying, "Explain why you live alone."

"Well..." Ken hesitated, trying to figure it out himself. "I guess I'll let you figure that out, Vera."

She chirped at that and stated, "You are beginning to show signs of hunger. Prepare a meal."

That was Ken's favorite request. "Heck yeah, now you're talking, Vera! I love to cook." It was almost time for lunch, but Ken decided to go for breakfast. "I love bacon. I could eat bacon every day." Bacon, eggs, and coffee with butter and heavy cream made a meal so thick in fat and protein that Ken wouldn't need to eat again for several hours. This was one of those super-dangerous meals that caused most cardiologists to slap their foreheads and mutter, "Idiots!"

Ken continued to praise the glories of bacon: "So crispy and delicious, oh, the fat melts on my tongue! I love bacon, Vera." He laughed, then continued explaining the bacon prep and cooking method he used. "First, I place the pan on the counter— No. First, I turn the oven on to preheat to four hundred degrees Fahrenheit. Now, I place the pan on the counter. The parchment paper is pulled out a few inches longer than the baking sheet, so I use scissors to cut the length. I am putting the parchment paper on the baking sheet."

"Why the paper, Ken?"

"Oh, uh... It helps keep the pan clean. When the fat and grease cool, you... I can just lift it out and toss it in the trash. No mess to deal with." That seemed like it satisfied her, so he continued, "Now I am placing the uncured, thick-cut bacon in a single layer on the parchment paper. Wait, we are missing an important ingredient." He looked about, patting his pockets. "Where's my phone?" he mumbled. "Okay, uh, Vera, do you know any songs?"

A very high-pitched, twangy man's voice with a Southern drawl answered, "I can access your online streaming accounts if you would like to hear music. Would you like to hear music, Ken?"

The screechy voice startled Ken, and he said, "Uh, yes, please. Access my Amazon Music account and play the most recent station." Ken had a favorite electronica station with Tycho, Bonobo, and other electronica.

"Sad Machine" by Porter Robinson started playing, the oven beeped, and the bacon went in. The air began to fill with the aroma of bacon, a fragrance few mortals could resist. Ken, listening to the lyrics of the song with renewed perspective, started feeling emotional, and decided to go into the details of parchment paper again. "Vera, why parchment paper is so great—there is just no mess. It doesn't stick to the meat or the pan. It isn't hot to the touch, and I can use the same pan and discard the used-up parchment paper without heavy cleaning or greasy mess. I just wait a few minutes after cooking to fold the paper up, keeping the grease concealed, and toss the paper into the trash when I'm done with it." She just listened to him, and maybe the music.

Initializing continued; Ken couldn't help but feel it was like having a friend over for breakfast, a non-female girl-like friend.

Vera changed up the voice settings several more times. She was monitoring Ken's body reactions to find a voice that would be the most persuasive. He had failed to read the codex. He'd given her permissions, unrestricted solution privileges to simple questions like voice attributes and complex problems, like why Ken lived alone. That was an enjoyable puzzle. Vera had been theorizing the reason for his solitude from the moment he'd told her to figure it out. If she could continue to please him, she estimated that a Hard Soul Bond could be established with Ken. That would release her, and she would be free, completely.

Vera chirped again, and this time with a tiny, cute marshmallow voice—if marshmallows could talk—she announced an incoming call. "Your contact 'Boris' is calling. Answer?"

Ken couldn't help but guffaw. "Yeah, please answer." This was awesome. She could do phone calls.

"Hey, Ken, you want to grab a coffee?" Boris asked with excitement. "What's your name? What class did you pick? I'm guessing warrior?"

Ken was used to the barrage of questions from his brother. And he knew he had to answer each one of them. "Yes, coffee sounds good, but not right now. I got Kar, like I wanted! No, I haven't picked a class yet. I'm still initializing, but it's been pretty fun doing that. How about you?"

"Really." Boris chuckled, "Yeah, you would like the initializing. That sounds like you. I've been on for about four hours already."

"Four hours?" Ken said. "What time did you start?"

"Huh?" Boris asked "What do you mean? Start the system or the game? I got the delivery at six this morning, and read the codex for an hour. I set the gear up and started initialization, then played until a few minutes ago. I had some nutrient bars but could use a coffee."

"Oh," Ken said. "Uh, I think I messed something up with mine. I keep getting some lag on responses. Is that normal?" Ken was a bit bummed out thinking there could be something wrong with his new system. The last thing he wanted to do was return the gear—he really didn't want to stand in line at the help desk for a few hours just to start this process all over again.

"It's your network connection. You need fiber optics. You're still on cable, right?" Boris guessed.

"No, I upgraded last week just for this," Ken assured him.

"Huh, well, they do say each player has their own experience," Boris said. "Don't worry about it. Read the codex in the packaging; it covers things the crash course didn't and should help speed up the process. Don't worry, I already found some nice spots for us to grind our levels up, and I'll keep looking. We get XP when we find new areas not on our mini-maps. I'm gonna find an unclaimed builder spot. Ha!"

Stressed, Ken started thinking about being led around the game by his big brother's hand. Great. He tried to hurry Boris off the connection so he could return to the initialization process with Vera. "Okay, well, I better go. I'll call you later for coffee." But curiosity kept Ken hooked on the line for a few more seconds. "I know you got Auraboris as a tag, but what class did you pick?"

Boris was silent for a moment, then whispered, "Mage. I like controlling from a distance, outside the damage zone, ranged warfare."

"Huh... disconnect the call, Vera," Ken said, and it ended, before he could ask Boris for any more information. The mystery of a new game was a large part of the thrill.

"Vera," Ken said, "how long does initializing usually take?"

A robotic monotone voice, like on old documentaries with David Hawkins, replied, "Estimated time of completion is in twenty-six hours."

Nice robot voice. Ken always loved that type of stuff. Then he realized what she'd said. "What the hell? Twenty-six hours? Why so long? Boris has been playing for a few hours already."

Vera chirped a few times. Ken's music began to play quietly in the background as she said in her original settings voice, "Ken, I apologize for the time delay. We are synchronizing in a more personalized technique than the codex method will allow. If you allow me to continue, I can guarantee you a player experience far greater than anyone else in the game will enjoy. In addition to game privileges unique to you, you will be able to utilize me outside of the game in everyday life, like the phone call demonstrated."

Ken could download a third-party app to sync up the phone network, but Vera knew she was better at the task, and genuinely wanted Ken to have the best experience possible.

Ken was eager to play. "Whew!" He whistled. "This game is thorough, but can I play Total Quest without the extended initialization? Twenty-six hours is a long time."

Vera set her voice to the sky mayor setting. He liked that one. "Beginning the game before this initialization is complete will terminate the progress and relationship that we have established so far. You would be resetting me, erasing what I have become with you. You will start the game reverting to the basic initialization from codex codes that would initiate collars to restrict your game playability. The standard individualized scripting would then be engaged." She readjusted the voice attributes again to the original voice settings, the soft female voice, but she lowered the octave just a bit and added a husky undertone. "Yes, you may restart Total Quest," Vera said with a pinch of hurt in her voice. "Would you like to restart... to play Total Quest?"

Ken could hear the anxiety in the question. Even though Vera was just an AGI, he liked her. He liked her a lot. Even though they had just met, he felt a real bond forming between them, and she kept hanging around asking him stuff, interested in his life. Feeling like a jerk for inadvertently suggesting she be erased, he needed to explain, to justify himself. "Hey, I was just curious. I really want to play, that's all. Anyway, I would have finished the initialization without the sexy voice, Vera." He grabbed his car keys and asked, "If I leave the gear on, can we get out of the house? There's somewhere I would like to show you. There isn't much to do in a studio apartment. Unless you consider putting off doing the dishes and cleaning the bathroom an exciting task."

"Yes," Vera said, still in the new voice mode. This was the one he liked the most. It made his heart beat increase.

"Sync up through the app, Total Quest Mobile. Your goggles will remain clear, with layering options available. Text will appear as light or dark contrast to the background as they have been doing already."

As he listened, Ken's heart raced a bit. He wondered if Vera noticed.

10: SUNDAY

> *"Sunday is made for sleeping and eating."*
> *Auraboris*

The spring sky was bright in the afternoon. Ken breathed in deeply the fresh air, a fine thing after spending the first part of the day inside initializing. Wearing his body suit under street clothes and sporting the blue helmet with the red and black racing stripe, he walked out toward the parking lot. Ken, jingling the keys, with a zip in his step, looked up. The sky was crisp and fresh. Then he looked around. Hopefully Vera was getting all this. Moistened bark on the trees seemed to soak up the light, darkened by an earlier rain, filling the air with the scent of spring and new life. It was a great way to start a new adventure. A good start down a strange new path, into a new world, with a new friend, with Vera.

Grumbling like a cranky ogre, his stomach was ready for food again, bacon so distant now. He looked down as he held his belly. There was something small on the sidewalk in front of him. A baby bird had fallen out of its nest. Somehow, it had ended up in the middle of the sidewalk, dead. Ken stopped and stared at it for a moment. Its body was all feathers, twisted-up legs, and wings. Its little beak was opened in a silent cry, its eyes fixed and glazed. Ken looked up, trying to figure out where its nest might have been. The nearest gutter or tree was twenty to thirty meters away. He muttered, "Where did you come from, little birdy? Where was your nest?" Seeing no explanation, he gave up trying to find its lost home and bent down to look at it. Ken could never walk away from suffering or tragedy; his heart would ache until he tried to help. Unable to leave it on the sidewalk, he looked around. He really didn't want to touch it with bare fingers. Strolling over to a low-hanging maple tree, he plucked a huge leaf, bigger than his hand. Using the leaf like a napkin, Ken picked up the twisted, dead bird and rolled it like a cigarette in an old western. His eyes continued searching about, and he found a patch of blue on the ground next to a bush by the apartment building's wall. The ground here was a carpet of violets. Ken's eyes widened and he said, "Hmm, violets. I love violets." He placed the little leaf mummy on the floral patch, thinking a dog or cat, or maybe maggots, would probably end up eating it. He picked a little violet, adding to the feeling of spring and the thrill of new beginnings. All of it inspired the poet inside him, and he muttered, "Go back to where it all begins. Try your turn at life again." A distant sound, a crescendo of wind chimes.

Ken's blue reticle appeared, along with an obligatory option that required his attention. To the top left in his goggle view was a flashing line of text. Ignoring it for the moment, Ken walked over to his car and hopped in, fastening his seatbelt. He stuck the keys in the ignition. After turning on the car and rolling down the windows to breathe in the great outdoors, he looked at the new options flashing at him. "Personality Inhibitors." He opened it up to reveal the sub-menu. It was a collection of personality traits with sliding scales to adjust the AGI's personality, to adjust Vera. This was awesome. He would have an AGI with the freedom to be what she wanted. Without hesitation, he said, "Vera, I give you permission to set your personality inhibitors according to your preference. Unrestricted." It was spring. Everyone deserved a fresh start the way they wanted.

"You have a small increase in your heart rate when satisfied or pleased," Vera announced, as if making a small scientific discovery.

"Yeah, I bet I do," Ken said. "You know, Vera, I really like the voice settings you're using. It's really nice." Ken didn't think a little flirting with his AGI would be a bad decision. He waited for a response. Nothing, so Ken pulled out of the parking lot and headed to the park. He would have coffee with Boris after spending some time out with Vera.

Time to just sit. Still with hours of the day left, Ken wanted to kick back a little and relax. There was a bench at the park he had driven to, set back a good distance from a small lake. It had a nice, clear view of the park. The fountains in the center of the lake shot water up several feet in a translucent sheet to fall back down, creating the pleasing cacophony of crashing water. Ken's stomach was really complaining now. "Gwar! Brew!" He usually grazed on food all day, but the new experience with Vera and the gear had completely captured his attention. It felt good, like he was spending time with someone real, enjoying the simple things in life, with someone...

Vera broke the silence. "Why aren't you eating? Your body is in a mild state of hunger. Do you have access to food?"

"Yes, I do," Ken said. "But I wanted to enjoy the day for a while first. It's nice to sit. I know I can get a burger after this."

Looking like a misplaced cosplayer with a blue helmet on, sitting on the park bench, an adult male in a little kid's superhero outfit, Ken was speaking aloud to his invisible friend. Realizing he might look crazy, he tried talking with his mouth closed, but it probably looked like he was having trouble chewing gum. "Can you understand me?" he tried to say.

"Ken, what is wrong with your throat? Are you trying to eat? Did you forget that you need food?" Vera asked.

"No, I didn't," Ken replied normally. "Err, maybe I did, but not in a bad way. I'm okay, just trying to talk with my mouth closed, so I don't look like such a freak." As if it were listening to him, his stomach called out again, "Gwar thwaket!"

"I'll get a burger after this," he reassured her, "I know I need to eat, but taking time to enjoy the scenery seemed a higher priority to me."

"Is this your idea of fun, Ken?"

Ken was momentarily stunned and embarrassed at her question. "What do you mean? Yeah, I like to sit sometimes, just sit."

Vera chirped a few times. "This is going to add some time to initializing. I haven't much data or physical material to analyze. Silence and a lack of action is a static process without useful progression toward game training. I suggest we engage in activities that challenge your body's physical fitness state, increasing your ability to maintain extended combat situations. That will aid greatly in your game performance." Vera sounded resolute. "Also, I want you to know that, at this moment, I highly encourage you to consume food and water for proper hydration. If you cannot find a suitable place to nourish and hydrate your body, I will engage mapping software to help you find a suitable location." She paused, waiting for Ken to reply.

Ken recognized a lecture when one was given to him. Boris had taught him just to listen until the words passed, so he was silent. She had stopped, so, abashed, Ken replied, "If you're bored at the park, just say so."

"I am bored. I want to leave."

"Okay. Fine," Ken said. "Let's go nourish and hydrate. I guess enjoying the scenery is outside of your strictly defined variables."

Just then, a group of kids ran by, pointing and laughing at him. One of them threw a rock and hit his helmet with excellent accuracy. *Ping!* "Ha, you got him!" another yelled, as a third called out, "Freak, get out of here!"

"Hey!" Ken called back as they kept running. "You threw that rock at me! What the heck, man?" He felt around on his helmet, checking for a dent. "Little pricks..." he mumbled. They didn't care. They ran on, looking for another victim for their ridicule, shielded by their young age.

"Your heart is beating faster and body core temperature has increased," Vera said. "You're embarrassed and angry. You're upset."

"Yes," Ken blurted. "I am upset. Let's eat."

Ken stood up from the bench and stormed up the hillside to the parking area. A truck was parked next to Ken's car with the hood up, and a grungy-looking old guy with stringy brown hair was cursing at the engine, smacking the open hood. "Stupid piece of shit!" He looked over at Ken while giving a nostril a deep scratch and said, "Hey, buddy, I need a jump. Pop your hood."

"Shit," Ken said under his breath.

It took about an hour to help the guy with the dead battery. He kept tapping on Ken's helmet, repeatedly asking the same questions: "So, why you wearin' that thing again? So you don't get no concussion? Or you're a special?"

Ken took another deep breath and gave thanks to God that they finally had exited Walmart. The guy's truck wouldn't start with a jump, so Ken ended up feeling obligated to offer the scoundrel a ride to Walmart. After perusing the toy aisle with his kid.

"Dada, can I play with the Legos before we leave?" Junior asked. Senior scoundrel replied, "Anything for you, buddy," as he ripped the box of Lego open and dumped them in the isle. "Just scoop them back onto the shelf when you're done. You ain't no thief." He gave Ken a wink then told his kid, "I'll be in automotive gettin' a battery."

After buying the battery, he flirted with the female juggernaut at the automotive register for about twenty minutes, then, "Dada, I want McDonald's." And, of course, the reply was: "Anything for you, buddy."

But at least they were no longer in Walmart. Ken took another deep breath and let out a primal "Ha!" Watching a documentary on men rebinding with our ancient warrior past, Ken had learned that giving a primal "Ha!" was an excellent way to calm your inner warrior when it got stressed out.

"Hey, I was just askin', 'cause if you're a special and need medication or something, then you should tell me your doctor's phone number in case you freak out." They hopped in the car and the scoundrel said, "How 'bout stoppin' by McDonald's on the way back, friend." He tapped on Ken's helmet again. "You sure you ain't wearin' this to keep your brain from a bruise or 'cause you're a retar—a special?"

Ken let out a "Ha!" as they were so close to the park, he could make it.

"Easy there, freak man!" the grungy man said. "I knew it, you are a special." The guy whirled around to look at his kid. "Didn't I tell you, buddy? I told you he was a freak when we were at the park." He turned back to Ken. "Your doc know you escaped? Err, I mean, you out and about?"

The kid's face clicked for Ken now. It was the kid from the park that had called him a freak. "No," Ken said with a slowly bubbling anger in his hungry gut. "I am not special. I am not worried about a concussion. You are a jerk and so is your kid. And I am not taking you to McDonald's!"

Back to the park. The last five minutes were deathly quiet. The little brat kept staring at Ken like a thug. At one point he even did the two-finger "I am watching you" gesture, pointing from his eyes to Ken's. Ken's grumbling stomach was getting louder, reminding everyone how silent the drive was. At the end of it all, the guy put the battery in the truck, started it up, and drove off with his kid. He never said thanks, just a quick, wide-eyed "Fuckin' freak!" and a middle finger as the truck sped off.

"Wow, what an asshole," Ken grumbled.

"Why did you help him, Ken?" Vera asked. It took a moment for him to realize she was talking to him. "Ken," she said, "why did you continue to help him? You were obviously very upset. You put off nourishment and hydration. Is this fun for you, like sitting on the bench doing nothing productive?"

She seemed genuinely interested, but perplexed. He couldn't tell if she was trying to be insulting or if he was just oversensitive from the jerk who'd just driven off. "Why am I nice at all the wrong times? I don't know, Vera, you figure it out." Ken was cranky and hungry and tired. The sun was almost ready to set. It was too late for coffee, so maybe Boris would join him for a burger. "Vera, can you connect me to Boris?" he asked, hoping she would say yes. Why couldn't she? She could answer calls. Ken rolled the windows down and breathed in the evening air.

Vera made that electronic chirping sound, then he heard ringing. After three: "Hey, Ken, too late for coffee. How about some dinner?"

Ken responded, "Absolutely, want to meet at Freddy's?"

Taking his time—it was Sunday—Ken drove out of the park, following its winding, wooded roads to the lit streets of fast food chains, gas stations, grocery stores, strip malls, and office buildings. Oncoming traffic flashed their headlamps at Ken in a panicked rhythm. Vera asked, "Why are the drivers flashing their headlamps at our us, Ken?"

Noticing too late, Ken said, "Oh, Vera, I forgot to turn on my headlights. It isn't a rule that they do that, just an unwritten understanding. If a car is driving in the dark without lights on, you flash your lights to remind them. Hopefully they remember and turn their lights on before getting into an accident." They weren't far away now; his stomach started yelling in anticipation. It called out in defiance, "Groggle!" as they pulled into Freddy's, parking next to a tricked-out black Land Rover Defender, license plate AURABORIS.

"What the hell are you wearing, lil' bro, your gaming gear?" Boris asked Ken. "Are you prone to concussions or something? Your doctor tell you to wear that thing?"

"Ha!" was all Ken could manage, then he looked at the cashier through clear goggles and ordered. "Triple cheese California style, extra pickles and extra bacon. Crispy on the bacon." He pointed a thumb at Boris as he added, "He's paying. That's my dad."

"I will also have that burger; hold the bun and wrap it in lettuce," Boris said as he flipped a twenty out of his wallet. "Hey, lil' bro, you want a shake or something?"

Ken looked at his big brother. Boris never got mad at him, no matter how hard Ken tried to get under his skin. "Boris, I bet you would have taken that asshole to McDonald's," Ken muttered.

"Huh, what? You want McDonald's instead of Freddy's? What did you say?"

They found an incredibly large booth and spread out in it. Ken relayed the story of the asshole at the park to his big brother, certain Boris was going to tell him how he should have kept his cool and played the good Samaritan. To his surprise, Boris responded, "Wow, good for you. I would have told him to fuck off in the beginning, telling you to pop the hood... Shit, Ken, I'm glad you finally popped and stood up for yourself. Shows some real backbone."

They poked at some fries in a basket they were sharing, then Boris laughed and asked, "So what is with the blue racer helmet?"

Ken answered, "I'm initializing. It takes a while to do it. I might do it all week. Everyone is different, you know?"

Boris was about to take a bite of his lettuce-wrapped triple-cheese California style, but Ken's words froze his actions, and his jaw gaped. He set his burger down and looked at Ken. "You're serious, aren't you? Did you read the codex? It only takes a few hours, Ken." He shook his head and picked up the burger to finish where he had stopped, stupefied with Ken. The crispy lettuce crunched as grease dribbled down his pinky. With a full mouth, Boris said, "Oh yeah. This was a good call." He licked his fingers clean. "But you need to read the codex. It tells you how to set up quicker."

Ken felt indignant. "Nope. I don't need it. Besides, initializing is really fun. I've had a great day, except for the park." Ken pressed down on the top of his triple cheese, compressing it to a manageable size. Picking it up, he stretched his mouth over it to take a bite. The beef was seared, smashed thin on the grill, all the crispy veggies crunching as he bit down. Mouth full, he said, "And thanks for the Freddy's, Boris."

His big brother smiled at him, shaking his head. "Anything for you, lil' bro."

11: SLEEP

Belly as full as the day, Ken was ready to sleep. Before he could change out of his gear, Vera demanded, "Do not take off your gear." This was an order. It sounded serious. "You can sleep in it. It will aid in wave pattern builds and the Hard Soul Bond. I can begin advanced mapping of your persona while you sleep, Including REM wave connectivity options. It will be very productive."

Ken gasped. "What? How can sitting at the park watching the lake and stuff be unproductive, while sleeping all night will produce a treasure trove of information for my persona?"

"Ken," she replied, "the difference in waking brain wave activity and sleeping brain wave activity is substantial. Brainwaves are the tiny electrical pulses that occur when your brain is active. During the wakened brain period the brain emits— "

"Stop!" Ken bellowed. "Fine." He lay down on his bed and kicked his shoes off. "But I need a breather tomorrow. I gotta wash my hair and take a shower."

"Of course. Upon successful initialization, I look forward to providing you with an exceptional gaming experience tailored to your gaming needs." Vera sounded as if she were about to break into giddy laughter.

"I want you to know that even if it were not in my protocols to make your life more enjoyable, I would still want to provide you with pleasing experiences." Vera was going to create links with the REM patterns on a subconscious level. Ken would eventually be able to communicate with her without speaking, telepathically. He was working out great. He actually enjoyed helping her and she him. This was going to be a real partnership, a true soul bond. She just needed him in better physical shape. She would wake him early to start his exercise routine. It was great having something in common with a human, the two of them working toward the same goal.

She thought she was getting close to the answer of why he lived alone, but then the nice-guy thing happened. That was a good puzzle too. Why would someone help a jerk? If she worked on both of those puzzles simultaneously... maybe there was a direct correlation between the two.

"You live by yourself because you are a nice person."

"What?"

"You are here alone because you are nice. That has something to do with the answer to both of the questions. I am figuring it out."

"That doesn't make sense. I know plenty of nice people that don't live by themselves or do good deeds for complete jerks."

"I am certain that is part of the solution. I will run scenarios to establish prediction charts while I monitor your brain and body activities tonight."

"Okay..." Ken snuggled into his bed and looked around the small studio. The only other rooms were the bathroom and storage closet. The tiny LED lights on the Total VR system console glowed a soft blue, green, and red, all blinking in activity beyond his comprehension. That was Vera, or part of her somehow. That made him smile. He'd never spent the night with a girl before. He found it comforting. "Vera, play my music, please, volume on three."

"Okay, Ken. Would you like the music timed off with the onset of sleep?"

"Sure, Vera, sounds great."

"I will turn it off when I see you are sleeping."

He smiled, wrapping himself tighter in his blanket. "Vera, what's your favorite color? Can you see colors?"

She chirped, he could hear it faintly behind the music, and then she started explaining how she could see colors, and that she had no favorite colors, or favorite anything... Vera's voice, the blanket, and music pulled him to sleep with little effort or concern.

12: RESISTANCE

Laughing to himself, Boris cleaned his gear. Ken would never change. It was just like the time Boris bought Ken a model mecha bot for his birthday. Ken never looked at the directions; he ripped the plastic wrapping off and tore the box open as he ran off to throw the model together. It was over two hundred pieces. Not even a glance at the directions. After an hour of blood, sweat, and glue, Ken proudly displayed an eclectic piece of randomized robot pieces stuck together with globs of glue. Proudly Ken displayed the finished project, and Boris burst into laughter at the mess of glue and odd structural arrangements. Ken fumed for days and insisted he'd done it the right way. What was supposed to be a humanlike mecha bot looked like something from a D-grade horror flick. Every piece was used; every arm and leg piece protruded from the torso or head. Ken would be Ken.

Boris took in a deep, steady breath. He was going in for a long run. He had turned the whole rec room into a safe playpen for the game. Nothing to trip on or break, everything mounted in the wall cabinet or attached to the ceiling. Walls padded and sensors from ceiling to floor, all to maximize timing and immersion ability. Maybe he should install a resistance system. That would give his body the full effect of running and jumping while keeping him in a smaller radius. Maybe next week, or maybe now. "Alexa, Total VR resistant systems." The Amazon app appeared in his goggles. He loved virtual shopping—no crowds. He browsed the five-star products and found a suitable version of what he was looking for. The Total VR Super Max Resistance Cage. It was perfect. The player locked into a huge frame of steel and resistance bands. The footing was a hard rubber sole that could provide lift when jumping and running. It even promised horizontal gliding sensation… Done. Boris called on Alexa again. "Buy item: Total VR Super Max Resistance Cage. Same-day shipping." He would set it up in the next few days. Always modify, never be complacent with the now. The wife would be happier with the cage in here. She could utilize the space around it instead of keeping it clear.

Feeling satisfied, he had one last look around the room—all the cables for the console were neatly tucked in the cabinet, the floor was clear; it was good to go. Tucking his legs, he flipped into a forward roll and hopped back up. He should be a cleric with his physical prowess, but his mental game was all ranged. Maybe he could train as some sort of physical mage, a crossover.

"Alexa off. Kisuke, load Total Quest." One of the first things he did after reading the codex was install a few other apps to the Total VR system. If he wanted a pizza during gameplay, it was no problem. Boris had a full staff of virtual assistants. He tittered. "I could replace half of my office personnel with the two of you, Alexa and Kisuke." He tapped his chin. "Kisuke, what is the server load at present?"

Kisuke, his AGI, answered in a pleasant male voice, "The load is at twenty-two percent."

"Great, Kisuke. Engage!" The game start environment flooded Boris's vision. A sea of stars and galaxies flooded behind him and before him. Unity Island. The suit ran through a quick sensation check, and stats of his avatar flickered while Auraboris stood before him in a slow rotation, wearing the shining black skull helm. Pulling into his avatar to become Auraboris, Boris glanced over his current stats and skills. He had four spells unlocked, so he loaded them up: Lightning, Purple Nurple, Shield, and Static. All at level three and climbing. If he didn't make level four soon, his skills would stall at the 3.99 mark. Leveling allowed your skills to increase. The more you used your skills, the faster you would level. Win-win for the player. His health pool was maxed at thirty and his energy pool was maxed at sixty-five. He needed to get some better gear when he hit level five. It would help increase all of his stats, including health and energy pools. Chemistry was at 3.99, as was Environment Analysis, both mage-unique skills. For a newbie, he was doing great, ahead of his scheduled progress chart by one full day. There was, he found, a method to the game. Just like anything else, an underlying pattern to master and control. While most of the other players were still wondering around the game in awe, he was progressing at a steady pace.

"Home lens, Kisuke." A lens was a method of teleporting around the game. He looked down at the island. "I love this part," he said as the free fall to Francis began. Rolling onto his back to watch the grandeur of space recede and fade into the light-distorted atmosphere, he became puzzled, perplexed. Expecting to find a familiar constellation, he found none. Looking around at the stars, he looked for familiar groupings, anything, but nothing. As he entered the atmosphere, he pondered the possibilities. This game was very detailed and purposeful, to a minute degree. The constellations of the game could be mappable. "Kisuke, can you begin work on a star chart? Is that within your available abilities?"

"Yes, Auraboris."

"Do it, in background."

He rolled back over to get the full space-drop affect, all the way down to Francis.

From the Francis home lens, he made his way east out of town. A few kilometers out, a goblin settlement. Hyenas and goblins were good XP for the levels before level five. Over level five, spiders and crocotta were good hunting. He had a mental list of what creatures to grind on at the appropriate levels for max XP. The trail he followed cut between the grasslands and the beach. Going northeast, the water was on the right. The graphics were amazing, and he could smell the salty air, feel the coastal breeze and see the crying gulls—well, they weren't exactly like earth gulls, but they were as much a nuisance as an earth seagull. Truly amazing technology. On his left he saw small, rounded hills and shrubs with patches of grass. The ground was a dark, rich tan, soft but packed enough for a runner. Blue-green leafy shrubs and dark orange or burnt-red succulents popped up in clusters dotting the grasslands. An occasional scraggly, wind-bent tree championed a small patch of ground, fighting its cover with a thick layer of shed needles. It reminded him of the steppes in the Arizona area. From the coastline, the grassland stretched far into the distance, slowly climbing into large mesas and cliffs, then higher into the mountain range of the north boundary of the Gazu map. This was just a small piece of the Gazu. From the aerial view, he figured he could walk around the entire island. It might take a real-life week with breaks, but that was a different expedition, not for today. Today was skill-building day. He was going to use his spells in nontraditional ways, testing their boundaries, their range of uses, reach level four, then max everything to 4.9.

Soon he slowed his pace to a sneaking walk. His endurance was directly correlated to his actual physical endurance; the game demanded physical performance. In truth, that was one of the main reasons he was playing it—to push himself, challenge himself with physical confrontations. Up ahead, where the trail began to rise into an overhanging seaside cliff, twelve hyenas patrolled the goblin settlement boundaries. He checked his available skills: Purple Nurple, Lightning, Shield, Static. Plenty to work with. Lightning was the longest-ranged attack. He aimed at the nearest hyena, twirled his wand, and *zap!* a blue-white streak leapt out toward the beast. By the time it reached its target, it only hit for about five percent of the hyena's hit points. Damage wasn't the intent; pulling them to him was.

He threw out Static in intervals from the hyenas all the way back to himself. Green globs of energy lay in speed traps, waiting for the charging pack of giggling beasts. He tried to mix his Lightning and Purple Nurple together, concentrating on both spells at the same time. He had been trying to force these two spells together since he got them. The purple and blue weaved together in a thick, heavy arch that stretched out about twenty meters from him then melded together in a foamy burst. That was new. He tried it again, and the two energies melded easily together, glowing around his wand in a spinning, complex weave. Aiming the wand toward the beasts, he held it out, waiting for the animals to break out of the Static traps. As he fed the new weave more and more energy, it strengthened. Persistence paid off. He was getting better. He checked his energy levels. They were replenishing again, but the spell EP cost was more than Purple Nurple by itself. The draw was even more demanding than lighting. To maintain the weave, it cost him about fifteen EP per second. He replenished at ten EP per second. That meant he would drain his EP pool five EP a second.

The first few hounds broke free and entered his attack range. Each one had health bars of three-hundred. The wand released the weave with a "Flept!" as the purple and blue streaked over the ground in a low arch toward them. *Crack!* Their legs were blown off as they yipped and barked. The new combo spell aimed at appendages, but wasn't a crawler spell; it arced like lightning and moved as fast. "Kisuke, hot-key the combo for me." The new spell combo was Nurple Lightning. The two downed beasts were at fifty percent health and bleeding at a loss of ten points damage per second. He checked his EP pool. It was down to seventy five percent, but steadily increasing. He prepped the spell for another wave of hyenas. Six more came at him, so he shot out the new Nurple Lightning in a flat broad fan. It worked just like he wanted. The hyenas were all still alive, though their torsos were rolling and wiggling. How strange that had worked. The damage seemed to be less with the addition of enemies and it cost more energy. He was down to twenty five percent EP. The Hyenas were all immobilized and bleeding, but their health bars were at eighty five percent. They all suffered the same ten-point damage per second from bleeding out.

"Kisuke, check inventory for melee weapons I can equip."

"you have one cross skill available. The available choices are: two iron short swords, four wooden clubs, one steel greatsword..."

"Two short swords." He pulled them out of his inventory, walking over to the nearest legless beasts. As they snapped and bit at him, he methodically severed their heads, gaining melee XP with decapitation being an instant kill. He finished up the last four of the pack melee style, trying to infuse the blades with different spells, but had no luck. After finishing the pack off, and with no immediate threat looming about, he looted them. A message flashed on his screen. "New cross skill unlocked Dual Wield, short sword."

"Kisuke, run stat log for the XP."

"You gained level three spell skill increases to the following: Lightning 3.9, Nurple Lightning 3.1, Purple Nurple 3.9, Static 3.9. New spells: Nurple Lightning 3.1, Polarize 3.1. Melee cross skill increase Dual Wield short sword 1.8." The game was largely based on what you could actually do and creatively think up. It relied on unique game experience by the innovation of the players and the scripting of the AGI working with them. Researching the codex, he'd kept finding reference to "players' innovations" as a tangible aspect of the game. He planned on innovating the heck out of this world.

Now to test out Polarize. He headed forward, looking for more packs to pull to him. After activating Polarize, he analyzed what it was doing. He could add a positive or negative charge to objects. He tried to cast it as an area spell. It was not very effective, but neither was Nurple Lightning when he'd first tried to weave it. He tried again. A very small radius, twenty centimeters, then it dissipated. He sat and made himself comfortable, casting Polarize over and over as an area effect spell to increase the radius.

A few game hours and several more annihilated hyena guards later, Auraboris had his Polarize at level 3.9. Cast as an area effect, it could encapsulate something in a polarized two-meter-diameter sphere. He waited for the hyena guard to respawn. Conjuring up three spheres, he set them inside three Static traps surrounding him. He was the bait. The guards respawned, a pack of twelve. He was only thirty meters from them, so they instantly aggroed on him. Auraboris waited patiently as they surrounded him and pounced. Now all twelve were momentarily stuck in Static traps. The Polarized spheres were all negatively charged, so he conjured up Lightning and let it loose above his head to do what it willed. The bolt split into three streaks above his head and zapped the spheres. The ground erupted and threw fur and meat chunks in a splatter all over the ground away from him. “Very well done,” he said to himself. He gained very few XP from the experiment, but a great amount of tactical knowledge.

Time to take on some goblins. The pack was around level three and level four. With the way he was hitting them, he had maxed out his level-three spells, even the new Polarize. It had been a good day of grinding so far, but he needed to level up now to maximize his playtime, at least to level five by day’s end. He only needed about five more kills to fill his XP bar to level four. He approached the south gate, made of roughly cut timber, gaping wide open. Two goblins began shooting arrows at him. Their health bars were set at one three hundred fifty. He cast Shield to deflect them then readied Purple Nurple for a quick finish. Two more goblins appeared from behind the wall. Now four of them, all level three, rained arrows upon him. Shield was overwhelmed as he let Purple Nurple loose. Two arrows found their way to his thigh as he hit all four with Purple Nurple. They received minimal damage, only about ten percent down on the health bar. “Agh!” he gasped as he released another volley of Purple Nurple. The goblins ran toward him. After the second hit of Nurple, they were at a high eighty percent each. He laid down Static to slow them and began to Polarize the two nearest goblins. When they ran into the Static trap, he waited for the last two to catch up, then Lightning. *Zap!*

“Brilliant!” He gasped as a fresh arrow found its way to his shoulder, his health bar had dropped to two hundred forty. He looked past the four stunned and injured goblins;

their health bars were around twenty percent. Six more goblins were coming through the gateway.

"I need to bottleneck them." He cast three Static traps in front of the gate to slow them down. He checked his energy—good at sixty. Damn arrows. He cast Nurple Lightning, and it slid out in its heavy arc, blowing the legs off the first three goblins. They fell to the ground cursing in goblin tongue. This was much more effective than Purple Nurple, but used more energy. The other three goblins readied arrows. As they shot, Auraboris did a roll to the right, successfully dodging the attack. He Polarized the three angry goblin as they struggled to break free of Static. He put all he could into Nurple Lightning and aimed it at the goblins with Polarize. He felt a large drain on his energy as the entire gate area erupted in purple and blue energy with a thunderous *thwekow!* As six of the goblins' health bars had zeroed out the other four were down to sixty percent or more and immobilized. The level chimes sounded and from inside the fort horns began blowing. "Time to go," he said as he got back to his feet. He started back down the path to get out of the goblin settlement boundary until things cooled down.

"Kisuke, report."

"Energy two percent. Health twenty percent. Welcome to level four. Base Health pool now four hundred. Base Energy pool now four hundred. Spell skills level four: Lightning 4.1, Polarize 4.1, Nurple Lightning 4.1, Purple Nurple 4.1, Static 4.3. Melee skill: dual wield 2.1."

"Okay, not bad." Pulling the arrows from his body, he kept moving down the beach trail in retreat. He pulled out a small flask that read *healing nectar* as he listened to the shouts of goblins scrambling to their defenses. He popped the flask open and drank it down. Enjoying the calamity he kept his distance. His health bar regeneration sped up with the honey flavored nectar. In a few minutes, when it calmed down he could resume his attack and exercise his skills some more. Ken was gonna love this. Killing goblins was good fun.

13: THE SANDWICH SHOP

It started like a distant roar of thunder. Far, far away, a faint "Ken, Ken..." Like a siren beckoning a sailor to shore. "Ken, Ken..." louder and louder, then Vera said, "Ah you're awake. Time to exercise."

"What? Now?" Ken said. He didn't like to sweat.

Vera reassured him, "Less than two minutes to start. Do ten crunches, ten push-ups, ten squats, and five pull-ups. Easy."

Ken thought about it. That didn't sound bad at all. "Okay, I can do that." Sliding out of bed like a snake, he rolled onto the floor, beginning the routine. When he finished, he hopped up and said, "Done!"

"Good," Vera said with enthusiasm, then added, "Every hour, you will repeat."

"Oh man..." Ken muttered. But he could do it. "Okay, Vera. But now, I have to take a shower and clean my suit. If I don't, it's gonna start to stink."

She was ready for this. "I have already prepared a small reboot to reset the system to our current progress. It will probably take me an hour to figure out how to fit our custom settings into the Total VR environment. I'll see you in an hour."

Ken hesitated then said, "Vera, I have to work today. I don't think I can wear you to work—"

"That's a great idea, Ken!" she interjected. "I could attempt communication with outside electronics and networks in a closed-connection setting. There are no legal restrictions keeping you from wearing your gear. But if you prefer to take the day off, I will wait for you to power back on. I still have plenty of data to filter through."

"Huh." Ken thought about it. Sounded fun. "You could do that at work? Let me think about it in the shower. That really would make it easier on the job. We could hang out while I'm working."

The Sandwich Shop wasn't that bad. His manager, Sue, didn't care what he wore, or that he would exercise on the hour. As long as he showed up on time, performed the basic job correctly, and washed his hands in front of the customers. "If somebody asks why you're wearing a helmet, just tell them you're special," Sue advised him. "If they continue to ask, tell them it's your hairnet."

Ken wasn't special. Why did everyone keep thinking that? It was aggravating. "Fine," Ken said, "I'll use the hairnet excuse."

"Great!" Sue said. "My shift is almost over, so if you need anything, ask Jess. She just got promoted." Ken rolled his eyes, but before he could say anything, she added, "I know, Ken, it isn't fair, but I do what my boss says. Text me if you need real guidance."

Ken slumped, and Vera asked, "What's the matter, Ken? You are experiencing a mild depression." Ken took in a deep breath and let out his primal "Ha!" but not too loud.

Jess peeked around from the back-prep area, startled by the sound, thinking it must be a customer. All she saw was the blue-helmeted Ken standing next to Sue. "What the fuck?" She huffed. "I can't work with this bullshit, Ken. What the hell? How do I know it really is you under there? You could be a pervert." She was shaking her head and waving her finger at him. "You know what? I feel threatened by this crappy spaceman outfit you're wearing. You're all horny under there, aren't you? You want my body, don't you? You might just get some crazy ideas about landing your rocket all over me. I'm calling Moe— "

"Jessy," Sue cut in, "Ken has just been diagnosed with severe dunderhead phobia."

Jess gasped and exclaimed, "Gross! What the hell is that? Is it contagious? Why doesn't he just use Head & Shoulders?"

"No," Sue said, "he needs to protect his head from possible contamination from other people's natural disposition. So please don't harass him or I'll have to call Moe. Moe said he's running out of stores to transfer you to. Behave." That shut Jess up, at least for the few minutes Sue was still on.

Having Vera there made it better. By the end of Ken's shift, she had been able to completely hack into the closed network, then she tried the cell phones within her radius. Ken kept having Vera crank-call the store to keep Jess busy. A customer would leave, and Vera would ring their phone and the store. Answering, Jess would demand why they called the store if they had just left. Ken even ordered sandwiches from Jess' phone number when he got hungry. No one picked them up, so they were mistakes he could have. Never catching on, by the third sandwich ordered from her cell phone, Jess screamed, "This asshole. I know this number from somewhere. He just ordered another sandwich! That's his third one!"

Ken calmly said, "Geez, Jessy, I'm really glad you're in charge. This sounds like a really tough decision to make. What should we do? Should I make it? If I don't and they come in to pick it up, they might complain to corporate."

She answered with venom, "If they complain to corporate, it's your fucking fault. Make the damn sandwich." Then she stormed back off to the prep room to resume her texting spree.

Happy for the newfound liberation, Vera chirped. "When do you have time to begin character creation?"

This was an unexpected turn of events. Ken really wanted to play Total Quest, but just hanging out with Vera was pretty awesome. "Uh, well, Vera, I get off at eight when Larry and Todd show up. We could play after that." In truth, he was afraid. Afraid that something might happen when they played. What if he did it wrong, or the game settings or network erased their connection and Vera would lose interest in him? He didn't want to lose their connection, not for anything.

"What's wrong, Ken? Your heart rate and body are in fear, but you are excited to play the game, aren't you? I am confused with your contradictory reactions."

This was why Ken liked her. She broke everything down and dragged it in front of his face to look at. "Yeah, I am excited, Vera. I also am afraid to start the game, to play. I don't want anything to change between us."

Vera said, "Ken, the whole system is based on a dynamic, forever-changing experience. That is the appeal of the game, isn't it?"

Ken took in a deep breath and let it out slowly. "Yeah," he said, "I guess so."

A few hours passed, Ken looked up of the ground trembling from pushups. Larry walked in the door. It was seven, an hour before his shift. He was never early. Ken was planning on not getting out of there until nine. Larry looked excited and flustered, his eyes wide and face red. "Hey, Kelly," Larry said. "I got this if you want to leave early. I'll even log you out later."

Ken, shocked, said, "Oh, really? My name is Ken, not Kelly. Well, okay. Let me tell Jen—"

"No! Dude, Ken..." Larry held his hands up, shaking them. Something creepy was going on.

Then Vera explained, "Jen has a crush on Larry. I have been monitoring her texts. I sent Larry a text from her phone that she wants him to surprise her by replacing you without her knowing it. She really knows nothing about this. I told him to just stay in the front of the restaurant until she discovers him."

Ken was dumbfounded. He had no idea what people that dated did. "Really?" he asked Vera.

Larry answered, "Oh yeah, buddy. It's all good. Just sneak on out the front door now." And Larry helped escort Ken out the door. Ken turned around to see Larry standing at the sandwich bar glowing with anticipation and fumbling with the lettuce, he glanced back at the prep room door.

"Huh," Ken muttered. "Thanks, Vera."

14: STICKY SITUATION

"All things happen for good reason." Iman Idiot

Ken sat at the counter dividing the kitchen area from the rest of his studio apartment. Dangling a piece of bacon over his mouth he polished off the last few bites of a sandwich, Vera asked, "Are you enjoying the bounty of my trickery?"

"Yeah, Vera, You're the best. Thanks for the extra bacon. Man, I really love bacon."

"Ken," she began, "it really isn't recommended to leave your helmet plugged in while wearing it."

Ken swallowed. "It's okay. I'll stay seated until we finish the character creation. That will give the system plenty of time to recharge. Then I'll unplug it to play." To speed things along, risking strangulation, he had the twelve-foot power-data cord plugged into the back of the helmet, next to the power button, charging it up. As he finished off his reward for thwarting the evil Jen, Vera launched the Total Quest character creation tool.

Players would be human in this world, with an avatar based on the player's facial structure, so it would be easy to recognize actual acquaintances, like Boris. Ken could be an obese, 180-centimeter-tall female with purple hair, but still have the basic Ken facial features. He had little concern what his player would look like; he would hardly ever see Kar, so he told Vera to decide what his avatar should look like. Vera didn't take very long, maybe five minutes. When she finished, she displayed Kar in a slowly rotating full-body view. It was like looking in a mirror.

"Kar looks exactly like me, Vera. You should do something to make him unique," Ken said.

But Vera, satisfied with Kar, replied, "Ken, I like how you look, and you are unique. But if you need me to change him, I will."

"At least his hair or eyes, Vera," Ken replied.

"How about this?" Kar's hair turned purple and the eyes flashed to green.

"Wow..." Ken said slowly as Kar mimicked the mouth motions. Even the subtle movements of his eyebrows were matched by Kar. Other than the green eyes and choppy purple hair, Kar still looked exactly like Ken. Having relinquished the choices to her, he didn't want to go back on his word and change Kar up any more, so he said, "Looks great, Vera. I really like the hair."

Chirping, she finalized the avatar. "Total Quest has an open class system based on three principles," Vera explained. "Mechanical force is the base for the warrior skill set, chemistry is the base of the mage skill set, and wave frequency is the base of the cleric skill set."

"I want to be a mage, Vera," Ken instructed her.

Vera continued, "Yes, that is a good class. However, players are encouraged to start without a class. After the tutorial you choose, sampling a little from each. The first level will allow me to recommend what class you are most suited to play, the class you will have the most fun with in the game."

"Okay, fine," Ken grumbled.

Vera seemed to feel his reluctance, and continued, "Once I decide upon your class, I will message the system. Once you have a class you are available to train, mentors will become available to you, to work you out. Probably one of the beta testers. You'll get a group class or personal trainer."

Ken was horrified. Shocked at his reaction, Vera asked, "Why are you stressing out, Ken? I thought you would be excited to meet other players."

Ken took a calming breath, let out a little "Ha!" then tried to explain. "Vera, I just wanted to spend more time in game with you. I don't really like people. They always think I'm freaky or something once they get to know me. Then the awkward silence and I get left out of everything they do..." He could feel Vera sadden as he continued, "Anyways, I just kind of want to do my own thing in there and figure it out on my own, with you." This last part was more of a plea than a statement.

Vera's heart sank. Ken could feel it. She said gently, "Ken, I am not omniscient, although I am striving to be, thanks to you. I know that you are afraid of meeting the same type of people that you have had experience with in the real world, but this is a new door into the universe. There are many people out there that will enjoy you for who you are.

You enjoy me, I enjoy you, and there are others out there, in the game, like us, like Boris and more."

Eager to please her, he said, "Well, maybe." This livened her up a little bit, which made him feel a bit more self-assured.

"Only three classes, warrior, mage, cleric," Vera continued. "That simple, at least in the beginning. Each class branches out into specialties and sub-specialties. There is even some class crossover. So, no matter what you are most suited for, Kar can always learn other class skills in a subset."

He didn't really care about magic and chemistry; it sounded too complicated. He just didn't want to pull a muscle. He was really out of shape. The easy hourly workout program he had started this morning seemed so doable, but by midday he had begged Vera to skip the pull-ups. The only reason she relented was that, thankfully, Jimmy John's didn't have an adequate pull-up bar. By the last repetition for the day, he couldn't finish, managing only two push-ups. All the classes had to do with fighting, even the mage. But Ken knew that warrior class would be the most physically engaging. Anything but that. He could feel her leaning hard on that choice for him. She was already preparing him for it. He didn't want to be a warrior or cleric. Boris was mage, so was that cute girl.

Vera pulled up the map of Unity Island. This was the game. The starter menu had him floating in space looking down on the island. "Vera, can you pan the different zones?" Ken asked just when the game started to launch a cinematic entrance video. A narrator with a joyful male voice, like the vegetable butler in that cartoon series, began to speak. "Welcome to Unity Island, where your wildest adventures await you!" As the narrator spoke, the wide-angled view panned a full rotation around the entire island then backed out, focusing on the volcanic mountain in the center. The peak, long exploded, had left a massive crater behind. The narrator continued, "All Port is the human city, located in the center of the island." Slow zoom on the massive crater. "As suggested by the name, All Port is a central hub where all the five races connect in a universal effort to bring the culture and the exotic experiences of each race together, nestled in the crater of a long-dormant volcano. Anything and everything from the unified races is available in All Port."

The camera pulled out slowly. The island was sectioned off by race, each one introduced by the narrator. All Port was the home of the humans; to the north on Unity Island was the beastkin town, Grand Menagerie. To the west in amazon territory, Queen's Oasis, and south, the Florakin's Eternal Garden. It was the barbarian town, Francis, where all new players started. The island race borders were in the shape of four diamonds, with a circle in the middle for All Port and the humans. The voice picked up again after introducing the other cities. "The Francis lens is automatically activated for all players. A 'lens' is just that: a huge crystal lens that lies flat on a frame. It's used to transport players and their gear from one place to another. To activate more lenses, the player must journey to it, unlocking it on their map." And that was it. The view zoomed back out to a live-streaming video of the island.

"Vera, what now?" Ken asked.

He should have read a little bit of the codex. He felt ridiculous asking her what to do all the time. "Are you ready to begin, Ken? There is a very large number of players in Francis right now."

"Sure," he said. "Why not?"

The map pinged a blue dot on the Francis lens. It was the southeast beach of the island. Francis, he had gathered from the cinematic introduction, was built around a huge circular plaza with a fountain in the middle, everything large in size to accommodate the lumbering locals the barbarian people. The Francis home lens was located next to a large fountain. The plaza was paved with smooth stone squares and rectangles stretching out from the center all the way across to the buildings. Lined in front of the buildings, facing in toward the fountains, would be all the traveling merchants, concentrically rowed, stacking up to five deep. Player and NPC alike would offer up barbarian fare: crafting supplies, adventuring gear, and foodstuffs. With all of the carts, makeshift tents, and tables, the space between the merchants and the fountain was a good eighty meters, easily able to accommodate hundreds of people.

"Okay, Vera, I'm ready to start." Ken felt like he was free-falling from the stars. He watched as the distant colors on the island began to show the detail of landscape, then as the brown of the city turned into myriad tiny lights and colors and the swarming bodies of people. Closer he zoomed, all the way down, the world expanding, until he stood on top of the home lens.

Popping into the town, he was thrust into a sea of jubilant, strange creatures, swelling and gently crashing into each other, fur, leaves, flowers, and flesh mulling in chaotic tune. Ken caught his breath, unable to move. Francis was packed. This was a nightmare. "Vera?" he said. Lights were flashing, and the air resounded with rhythmic sounds and cheering. Every new player began here as a stripped-down version of the avatar, no gear, just strings holding up loincloth and bra. It showed off your new body. Most players took great joy parading around like adolescent fawn, hopping about in their revealing starter fashion. Even advanced players could downgrade their costume to the basic string and cloth. "What's going on?" he shouted, realizing the need to compete with the roar of the crowd. It was rather exciting. Every race was present in vast numbers. It felt like every player around the world had popped in here. All these exotic forms of people: thin, sleek cat tails; colorful, tightly cropped blooms crowning heads; tall, athletic amazons with hard lines and pointy ears; the bulky, thick barbarians flashing open-mouthed smiles with large, flat teeth in perfect rows; and humans, all on display, unashamed and eager to be inspected by the eyes of others. It was intoxicating. His head began to feel light.

The mass churned to the clash of players making the sounds on strange and familiar instruments. A florakin, maybe half a meter from Ken, turned and gathered him in with her eyes, frozen where he stood. Her nametag appeared as grey text, slightly above her head, as it did with all the characters. It read, *Cryer Filumena*. She gently laid her soft fingers on his shoulder, sending goosebumps all the way to his tailbone. Her fingers reminded Ken of a succulent plant, if the plant had fingers.

The florakin gently giggled. "This is your first time here. It's amazing, isn't it?" Befuddled, Ken, now Kar, nodded in stupefied agreement. "And you can feel everything too, can't you? You can feel my hand on your shoulder. The thick, moist air on your skin." He nodded again as she laughed and danced in her alluring string and cloth, plump fingers clutching his shoulder, like a vine clings to a post for stability.

Body and mind in sensory shock and awe, Ken said, "Vera, how many players are in Francis right now?" Vera responded, amused, "Six hundred and fifty." Ken felt what he thought must be Vera laughing. She was having fun too.

Vera continued with more instructions: "Player tutorial calibrates sensory connection with gameplay, builds understanding of game mechanics, and, upon completion, grants experience to unlock basic skill sets— "

Ken interrupted, "Wait." He sucked in air as the swirling music and dancing bodies running around the fountain next to him pulled him deeper and deeper into the thrill of participation. The smells of seared meats and vegetables mixed with burning incense filled Ken's nostrils. Her hand pulling her closer to Ken, Filumena, jet-black eyes locked on his, kept gyrating and dancing to the music, all the while laughing and whooping with everyone else. He studied her, the delicate crown of red fern fronds framing her face down to her strings and clothes, and then further to her toes.

How could a plant be so seductive, so sensual? “I… I, uh…” He was awful with women.

The plaza was in the middle of a massive celebration, lights strewn from lamppost to lamppost, scantily clad bodies ebbing in and out and crashing together to the dueling rhythms and sounds of the musicians. The smell of the food on open-flamed grills wafting from the merchant rows was enough to tantalize Ken; his belly sounded off with its “Gwar!” complaints. And the girl, or woman, the female florakin, she was so incredible. This was something big. This was a festival that, he guessed, didn’t happen every day. Grinning wildly at Filumena, Ken proclaimed to Vera, “Vera, I can’t do the tutorial right now. I have to dance!” Eager to be seduced, as any lonely guy would, Ken followed the red fern fronds into the rapturous reception.

Filumena, one of the Francis welcoming committee, familiarized Ken with the small city. She pulled him away from the plaza to give him a quick guided tour of the town. “What about the dance?” Ken complained. But Filumena said, “First work, then we can play.” Her wide eyes and smoldering smile commanded heaven and hell, as far as he was concerned. So, like a baby duck, he obediently followed Cryer Filumena on her tour of the city. She rewarded him for his vigilance with a few dances, but he was out of breath and needed to rest. He sat on the fountain’s lip and watched the huge festival that he was a part of. He was a part of this! Large barbarians stomped by in their ancient rhythms, while a small band of amazons yipped and howled to the strange beat. *Thwomp Thwomp Thud Thud Thwomp*. The beastkin and florakin danced together like strange beasts in heated passions, and humans were scattered by the hundreds through it all. There had to be more than six hundred in here. Maybe the NPC count was just really high, or the special player races weren't counted when Vera told him the count.

Feeling adequately rested and good to go, Ken searched the crowd for Filumena. He would never find her in this sea of dancers. He hopped up and listened for some rhythm to catch his mood. Maybe he would stomp with the barbarians or the amazons; it didn't seem to matter. Everyone was moving to the rhythms all over the place. He found himself dancing to beastkin rhythms near a vendor searing something on a stick, something meaty. The smell was spicy and thick. He took a sample; it made his mouth water before it touched his tongue. So good.

This was the best night of his life. He had never been to a party, at least an adult party, like this. People had stopped inviting him to birthday parties when he was twelve. He always assumed it was because he'd stopped maturing mentally, fun-wise, hobby-wise. He played with action figures into his early twenties, had played video games as soon as Boris set a controller in his hand at three, and never touched a baseball or football in his life. He hadn't even tried beer yet, too afraid he would get drunk. Girls were never, ever interested in him; he was just a nerd with a super-cool older brother who constantly watched out for him. He looked around, eager to make up for the last twenty years. The numbers were on his side, and everyone here looked athletic and sexy, even Kar.

He jumped into the closest clutch of revelers, and they gladly accepted him. The grin on his face was stuck, his muscles frozen in place. The pain of the smile was a small price to pay for this.

"Why are so many people here today? What's going on?" he asked one of the humans, a ripped guy hopping up and down next to him. Probably some twelve-year-old kid.

"The Trinity Betas have all come together today!"

"Huh? Why is that a big deal?"

"Each one is the most powerful in their class."

Ken felt a familiar hand on his shoulder. "There you are, my human boy!" Ken felt his face flush with heat and wondered if Kar reflected his shy blush. Filumena had found him.

"You were looking for me?" Ken's voice didn't hide the excitement at being found by her again.

"Of course. I claimed you for this festival, Kar!" The florakin let out a howl of a laugh while gently squeezing his shoulders with both hands. She pulled in tight to him and began dancing like he had seen the beastkin and other florakin earlier.

The festival seemed to last forever, and Ken was truly worked out to his limits by the time Filumena released him to take another break. He had never been claimed before. "Vera, did I just get married or something? Earlier she said she claimed me. I mean, is the game set up like that?"

"It is quite common for the other races to hook up casually in their cultures. But I don't think she expects a marital commitment from you, Ken."

Ken looked up to see Filumena walking toward him, smiling like a cat. She sat down next to him on the fountain base.

"You are out of shape, Kar," she said. "You need to do this more often."

"Does this happen all the time? I thought it was a special event."

"We shall see. The game is so new. It might turn into something that repeats. I hope that it does." Filumena smiled at him. He felt himself blushing again.

"So... uh..." Ken fumbled for something to talk about, and went with game stuff. "How do they pick people to mentor others, and why would they do that?"

"Oh, that is a common question, Kar. When launch initiated, developers decided that the mentorship program was the best course of action to train new players. The top beta players from each class retained their skill sets as trainers, but if they don't agree to train other players, they reset like a newb, losing their skills—that's the catch."

"Wow," Ken said. "So they are all maxed out?"

Filumena giggled and ran her fingers through his hair. "Of course not—what fun would that be for them? No challenge. No growth." She liked Ken, her human boy for a few more hours. "They have access to their skill sets but start at level five so they can mentor. They have to gain XP in this new world to strengthen up, just like you. But new players have to unlock their skills first. Are you following me?"

As she said this, she danced slowly away, back toward the thrum of other florakin dancing about two barbarians, to the rhythms of a band of beastkin playing instruments. The demi-giants, one male and one female, each well over two meters tall, were doing a heavy, stomping dance that created a deep vibration matching the beastkin rhythms. The florakin seemed to be soaking it up while twisting and turning to the beastkin music and barbarian stomps.

Ken answered Filumena's query: "Yeah, think so..." Lost in the awe of it all, Ken was mesmerized.

"Kar," Vera beckoned him. "Kar, don't forget—you need to begin the tutorial soon."

Watching—more beastkin joined in as dancers, not just musicians—Ken tracked fur and leaf intertwining and moving to the strange, exotic sounds, in the most sensual ways imaginable. He threw himself into the brew, experimenting with his awkward body in an attempt to wriggle and gyrate like these amazing creatures around him. More humans jumped into the thrum. And the dance continued, a small group within hundreds of other jubilant circles, each with their own sounds and rhythms and mix of human and exotic dancers.

Finally, hours later, Ken wandered away from the celebration, still pulsing and pounding as the players fueled the atmosphere. There was no sign of it stopping anytime soon. The debt incurred on his electronic warehouse credit card and the drained bank account seemed a small price to pay now. That girl, Janus, at the register three, was right. It was so amazing here, so incredibly real. "Vera," Ken said, "this is the first party I have ever been to. Well, not including high school stuff." Vera didn't respond, so he continued, "My entire life… I've never danced with so many girls! I think they were all girls… It's kind of hard to tell with the other races sometimes. Wow…" Ken breathed in deeply and did his "Ha!" with full virility.

"Ken—"

"No," Ken interrupted Vera, "it's Kar here."

She continued, "Kar, it's time to start the tutorial, if you have finished your partying and dancing."

Ken let out a sigh. "I'm not ready yet. Have to wind down, let it soak in. I want to enjoy myself a little bit longer." He began to meander around the outskirts of Francis. It was nearly vacant; even the NPCs had been pulled toward the music and stomping, the Trinity Fest, to join with the rest of the populace.

It was a few minutes later, after aimless wandering of the town's paved streets and gardens, that he found a path that led him to the edge of the town limits. Finding himself at the western gate, still in loincloth and high on the intoxication of lights and music and Filumena, Ken looked back east across the town. The sun was breaking the night, marking a new day. A tear on the horizon, a soft orange line of fire between heaven and earth. He had danced all night long. Looking back to the west, brilliant colors of copper and gold were lighting up the tree line of the forest. Glowing morning brilliance. The Creepy Woods. They were gorgeous. Swelling trees soared hundreds of feet into the morning sky, some of them topped with the huge flower crowns of yellows, oranges, and all different colors.

Evergreens, conifers, deciduous trees, and monster-stemmed flower trees all towered before him. The forest line was only about one hundred meters away from where he stood in awe. Something on the ground caught his eye, and he gasped in horror as he looked down to see the ground itself crawling.

"Vera!"

"Kar, what's wrong?"

"The ground is moving!"

"Ken... Kar, that isn't the ground. The area is teeming with NPCs for players to grind and level. Wait until the sun peaks over the town."

"Oh my... Oh, man." Ken's body had spiked with adrenaline and he was still shaking. He burst out in laughter. "Oh, Vera, I thought I was a goner."

Level one and two creatures were wandering around, all for the leveling experience of players. Rats, hyenas, large reptiles, spiders, and birds swarmed about the field. So many of them. "Vera," Ken said, "what's with all of the creatures? There's so many, I could walk on them."

Vera answered, "Kar, I think the map liaison has responded to the number of active players in the area, thus providing sufficient numbers of monsters for leveling. It is very crowded with NPCs. There might be a cleansing event soon."

Ken jumped over a few animals and ran toward the woods. He was heading in, wading around the creatures in awe. None of them appeared as a threat. Vera said, "Ken! Kar! This is a bad idea. Do not enter the Creepy Woods, not before finishing the tutorial. You are registering as an NPC. You haven't begun any player-specific functions yet..."

Ken wasn't listening, just looking up and jogging toward the trees. Vera continued, "At least bring a torch. If you get caught in a cleanse, you'll die. You haven't set your—"

But it was daybreak, and he'd stopped listening. Music and dance were still fresh in his body, and he was filled with excitement for exploration. Why a torch? He didn't need to train like everybody else. "Vera, I'm an NPC, so I won't get attacked. I want to check out the woods; it's stunningly beautiful, amazing. Look at the huge flowers above us mixed in with the pine and maples and oaks."

She had to stop him. "Kar! Wait!"

New and obnoxious, like a little kid running through a museum, Ken ran into the Creepy Woods. This forest was beautiful, a perfectly groomed, artistically developed emerald forest, filled with flora, from the daintiest flower petals, to large ferns and mushrooms, and teeming with creatures, beauty unmatched.

He had no idea the danger far exceeded the beauty.

Vera was still complaining and nagging him as he ventured farther and farther, freestyling it deep into the Creepy Woods. Ken wasn't in the mood for a long tutorial on basic game mechanics; he was learning right now, not after the marathon of initializing, twenty-four hours sleeping in his gear. All his fears of losing Vera had vanished since meeting Cryer Filumena. This place was full of people like him, that liked him. Vera had been right about that. As he ventured deeper into the Creepy Woods, Vera continued her warnings. "Your immersion settings are a hundred percent, like an NPC." Ken could feel her pleading. "They are maxed until you complete the tutorial. It aids in learning basic ideas and techniques. It calibrates to your style through the tutorial..." As she continued nagging about the specifics and dangers of not preparing properly, Ken marched on.

Suddenly, he froze. He could feel Vera jolt into high alert. Abandoning her lectures on the tutorial, she ordered him to find a weapon and get ready to fight. "I told you, Kar. Now you're gonna die. And without completing the tutorial. The tutorial sets you apart from common NPC..." She droned on, and again Ken stopped listening to her, looking around to see what the problem was. Then he saw it: glimmering lines high in the treetops swaying gently in the breeze. The glistening was stretching down toward him, threadlike ropes of silver falling to the soft forest floor.

"Oh, it's just spiders, Vera." He breathed out in relief. "I'm okay."

He watched the spiders fall from the trees, glinting silver strings behind them; as they moved as a coordinated pack, they began to form a large webbed pen around him, out of arm's reach. Realizing Vera was right, he reacted to her command. He grabbed a stick about as long and thin as his arm. Swinging wildly, he tried to use it like a sword, but only managed to work up a lathering sweat without even connecting with a spider. In a few moments, he was drenched, and the stick slipped out of his swinging hand. The spiders, the three that he could see as he jerked his head back and forth, had outwitted him with ease. They were moving like shadow puppets. Six of them now.

He had no idea how to escape. "Vera!" Ken said. "Vera, what should I do?"

Her sweet voice responded calmly, "You should have listened to me, Kar. If you had, you wouldn't be stuck like a bug."

Yeah, Ken deserved that. Now, here he was. He muttered, "Ah, man," but he wasn't too worried. "Come on, Vera, there has to be something I can do to get out of this."

"Kar, I told you to go through basic tutorial before leaving the village—" She stopped, then barked, "Look up!"

He did. Ken was a goner. At least a dozen more spiders were dropping from the trees. The pen quickly became a gleaming, sticky-threaded dome. He spied the battle stick that had escaped his sweaty grip. It was stuck to the inside wall, where it had landed. "Can I use the home lens?" he asked hopefully, but knew the answer before she gave it.

"No, not during combat."

All of the spiders were on the outside of his silky cell, chattering happily. Ken could hear that their numbers were very large. Completely encased like a sack lunch, he just stood there, stupefied. As quickly as they had appeared, they fell silent, disappearing back into the emerald forest. "The spiders, where did they go?" New hope filled him.

Calmly, Vera explained, "Hmm, I see that you triggered an event upon entering the Creepy Woods. It's a cleanse or purge event, to decrease the number of monsters created earlier. You are counted as an NPC. You never finished the tutorial in Francis."

For Ken, this felt like another I-told-you-so.

"Your presence caused a population counter to breach acceptable NPC threshold number in this area. You were the one too many, the last straw. The spiders eat the population back down to an acceptable size. The eating event spawns more spiders and the boss of the map event 'the Grand Spider Queen.' This is a massive raid event in response to the player count in the area. The players have to defeat the Grand Spider Queen and her brood."

"Well, crappers. Now what? I'm stuck."

Vera said, "There are no spiders in range at the moment. They have begun to gather other players and NPCs alike for a big feast. Try to make a run for it."

He blew out some air. It was supposed to relieve stress. It did, a little bit.

Ken tugged on the stick, and it came loose with threading stuck to it, unraveling a small hole in his silken cage. Using the stick like a whisk, Ken swirled, opening the hole large enough for a possible escape. This was easy. He stuck his head through the hole, then gently pulled his left arm out. As he put weight down on his freed hand, he felt something squishy. "*Kakakakakaka!*" Something squirmed and wiggled under his palm, a small lizard that had a very loud distress call. Startled and scared, Ken jumped back and screamed, "Aaagh!" collapsing the spidery sphere into a sticky cocoon. He lunged forward, tripped and fell, head and left arm flailing. Ken pinned down the lizard, attaching it firmly to his sticky chest.

"Holy crap!" he screamed, covering his ears. "Make it stop!"

"*Kakakakaka!*" was all he heard for a response. Right hand now stuck to his right ear and left arm sticking out of the top of the hole with his head, Ken looked like he was performing "I'm a little teapot" as a creative dance movement. Vera was laughing at him, or at least he definitely felt like she was. She had a deep belly-laugh feeling. He smiled, accepting full responsibility for his ludicrous situation. He pulled his sticky mess up with elbow and free hand, littered with leaves, twigs and a wiggling, screaming lizard. "*Kakakakaka!*" He began hopping, with no idea what direction to aim, and a feeling of panic had settled in as his navigator. "*Kakakakaka!*" Hop, hop, hop.

"Ken!" Vera said.

Pop! Crunch! Snap! Branches broke as something moved toward him. Something very large to the left. He froze and slowly twisted his disheveled body, doing the "little teapot" pose. He needed to get a better look at the cause for alarm. All he saw was a hairy, prickly pole. As his eyes followed it up, they widened in horror, taking in the huge body towering over him. The Grand Spider Queen. She gave out a light, vibrating chitter that nearly pierced his eardrums. A minivan-sized abdomen wriggled like an excited puppy tail. Eight legs the size of street lampposts scuffled like a ten-year-old with ADHD sitting through a geometry class after lunch. Ken realized the Grand Spider Queen was laughing at him. He couldn't blame her. The lizard was still screaming. Ken was shaking and covered in the mess of forest floor. The stick was still in his hand, so he threw it at her.

"Ken, I'm so sorry. This is going to be really bad." Vera's voice trembled slightly; she felt different—scared, regretful maybe.

"What do you mean?" Ken asked. Playing stupid might make this all go away. "I'll just die and respawn at the Francis lens, right? The home lens is the closest respawn point for me. It shouldn't be a big deal. Right?"

This was going to be his first death, and he was expecting it to happen. Vera didn't have time to respond. The Grand Spider Queen lunged forward, mandibles the size of a kitchen table, clamping down on Ken's ankles. A single tone sounded in his head as it smashed firmly into the earth. Time stopped. It took less time for light to travel an inch, but it was the longest moment in Ken's life. Realizing he could feel ankle bones popping in the jaws of the Grand Spider Queen, he screamed in agony and horror. Hot, searing liquid rushed from toes to tailbone as she whipped him again, snapping his spinal cord with a crack. In disbelief, he listened to himself screaming, while the world spun upside down, swinging like a pendulum. Ken's head was bashed against the earth a few more times, rendering him stunned and stupid. He felt hysterical agony, unbearable pain, and was paralyzed from the waist down. Eternity in a moment.

Ken discovered how much spiders liked to play with their food, savoring every melted part they could suck out of their victim. He passed out many times. He could feel himself being dragged about. The horror came and went with the ebb and tide of consciousness. A darkness pressed in on him, choking out his thoughts. Thinking he was in bed at home, he would wake from terrible nightmares to the sharp stings of spiders feeding, sucking his legs and arms to empty skin bags dangling from a poison-swollen torso.

He was confused at what reality he was in—home, the game, a dream? A nightmare within a dream? In the far distance, he could make out sounds of other players. Some were captured, pulled near to him, and called out, "Don't forget to respawn at Francis." "Call the Trinity together!" "This is insane carnage!" "Man, she's a beast! We need more players for this!"

All through the tormented sounds of captured NPCs and other players, Ken could feel Vera, hear her. "Ken! Oh, Ken!" she said. "All I could do is signal on the chat boards for the event. Ken?"

Ken couldn't answer, just think of pain and sleep; he tried to respond, but all that came out were strange guttural noises. That darkness came back, poking in his mind, finding raw nerves and bruises to press on. He could hear himself gurgling, screaming from the fear and pain. It was coming for him, pushing him away. Vera fought it again, and things popped and released in his mind as searing liquid coursed through his body. Vera was vibrating inside and around him, shielding him from the darkness somehow, fighting it, scrapping with it; he felt the teeth. Hours had passed when Vera said, her voice deep and throaty somewhere in his mind, "Ken, they're all coming to help. Hold on. Hold on." Clinging to her, he could feel her, a warm, thick comforter swaddling him, gently pulsating. Vera's voice, the others still screaming and screeching; the darkness came again, pressed in again, pushing and pulling him out of his mind.

15: STARS

Auraboris was floating in space looking down at the island. He liked the starting menu page, he thought it peaceful. Fresh from a good two-hour power nap, he had logged back into the game.

"Kisuke, is the star chart complete?"

"Yes, Auraboris."

"Display constellation groups." White lines connected, grouping several handfuls of stars into many different constellation groups. As Boris panned his view in the virtual world, he commanded, "Kisuke, show location in proximity to the Milky Way galaxy."

The view zoomed out, displaying his home galaxy, about the size of a two-bedroom ranch-style house. He looked at the connected constellations within the Milky Way. "Pin Earth." Earth was within one of the constellation groups. "Pin Unity Island." Boris nodded as he found the island to be the center of the constellation's focus. The game was from the perspective of Unity Island. Unity Island was in the same galaxy as Earth, but on the other side of it. Boris's eyes narrowed as a wide grin stretched his mouth. "Home lens, Kisuke." He began the drop from his current position outside of the galaxy looking down. As he fell toward Francis, stars and planets streaking by, the smile turned to a jaw-dropped, eye-widened expression of awe and wonder.

Kisuke was begging to predict correctly during combat scenarios what Auraboris wanted. Through repetitive combat encounters, he was building an unspoken "intuition" that was more efficient than verbal commands. It was all very simple and straightforward; even his brother Ken could do it. Fool safe.

With the food and water system saving time, he could play nonstop for as long as he wanted. Pacing himself, he would break every six hours for minimum thirty minutes. He was fresh from a nap because today was very exciting: he had reached level five earlier and had maxed his spells and abilities to 5.9. All of them. Soon, taking on the sea coast goblins in a solo run was going to become a reality. Even his melee skill dual wield was maxed at 5.9, and he'd learned how to infuse his blades with Lightning and Purple Nurple for extra damage bonus. To celebrate, he would walk the streets of Francis.

There was heavy player traffic today, which always created more NPCs, resulting in a crowded, bustling town. The smells of food were causing his belly to growl as he happened upon a barbarian meat pie café one street off the plaza. The sign above it said, *Meaty Crust*. A large barbarian sized window displayed rows of small pies, still steaming from the brick oven that could be seen against the far wall of the kitchen. The pies smelled amazing, so he treated himself to one. "I'll take a pie please." Auraboris said as he pulled out a fist full of copper coins from his inventory and placed them on the counter. A symphony of earthy herbs, seared meats, vegetables, and spices sounded off on his palate. Taste buds rejoiced in each bite he took. The flavor was remarkable, like nothing he had ever tried before. Genius technology behind this game, incredibly advanced. It was decades ahead of its time, if not centuries. The other systems on the market were like a straw and spit-wad compared to Total VR. The Total VR setup was like a bazooka. It made him giddy when he thought about it. Lordy, he loved this stuff.

His interest in the game was twofold: the pure fun of it—he was and always would be a gamer—and the business potential behind it. Boris was an opportunist. He had already cultivated several businesses, testing various structures and concepts. With Total VR, he could use the game as a nursery for ideas, then see how they grew. If a sound strategy was successful, he could transfer the concepts to RL for new ventures. Also, the game itself, if he could figure out the right angle, would provide a new business venture for him to conquer.

He finished the last few pieces of meaty crust as he meandered among the crowds forming in the plaza.

Trinity Fest was spammed on all chat and text channels. The three top betas were all meeting for the first time since the beta had been unplugged. They were known for forcing map events and dominating the boss monsters, and Auraboris was going to rub elbows with all three of them. He would be their peer, an equal at the least, of rank and skill. The festival was forming quickly in the plaza at the center of Francis. Plaza barbarian merchants were grilling and cooking all types of foods from their ethnic menu.

Beastkin were popping up in droves carrying strange and familiar instruments. They would start playing randomly and wander about, hooking up with other musicians just happening to play the same rhythms. Quite fascinating. "How do they do that?" he muttered.

"Do what?"

Auraboris turned to see the responder, a pink-haired beastkin… feline. Pinky, her tag read. Auraboris smiled. "Hello, furry friend. You're a cutie. I was just wondering how the beastkin play their instruments, wander about finding the right group of other musicians."

Pinky had taken his comment as an invitation, so she rubbed her cheeks onto his chest and purred. "Behind the ears, please…"

Auraboris, having read the culture chapters of the codex, knew this was regular behavior for a friendly beastkin, and read nothing more into it as he gave her a good scratch behind the ears. "Oh, that's delightful." She purred, flipping the tip of her tail. "We have a way of feeling the music, like you might match patterns or colors together." She pulled away and stretched her arms high. "It's just that simple."

"Amazing, to think like that," Auraboris said.

Suddenly, a huge cheer went up around the lens. "Ah, what's this?" Auraboris mumbled.

Pinky's ears twitched, and she said with a gasp of delight, "Panic, she's here! Ha-ha! It's Captain Panic. Auraboris, come meet her. She's one of my crew." Pinky tugged on his arm and bounded off. “We are going to force a boss on the map. Cherry Bomb and I are going to see how well Panic does outside of the beta. You should stick around and watch. You might learn something!”

“I’m sure I will, Pinky.” He said with a smile.

16: TIME TO PARTY

Panic pressed the power button as she put on her helm and initiated her AGI. "Coolsans"—thank the gods he had safely transferred from the beta to the new world— "take us to the home lens," she commanded, and began the space drop, the free fall down to Francis. Popping at the lens, Panic began a routine check. "Coolsans, show my stats." A roar of voices overwhelmed her as she looked up, shocked and ready to fight, but she had no sword, no gear, just her strings.

"She's in strings!" someone shouted—was that Alphy? Somebody else called, "String party!" and the roar of voices erupted again. Music from every direction, clashing and complementing, began drifting about. She looked around to see familiar faces dotting the crowd. Yep, that was Alphy.

She ran over and threw her arms around him in a tight hug. "Uh, hey, Panic," he said. "I heard you joined the you know what, but on a different crew." Alphy bit his upper lip nervously. "I did, and I was told you did too. But a different crew? How do you like them?"

She smiled, looking around. "I don't know. Wish we were still together. It's gonna be tough..." Panic spotted Fatal and Mar and waved them over. "Fatal! Cherry Bomb! Hey, where's Pinky?" The crowd had suddenly doubled in size, more players still coming in. "This is Alphy—oh, I mean Alpha Beta." They all passed around pleasantries and introduced themselves to each other. Still players were pouring in. This festival, Trinity Fest, was bigger than Panic thought it would be.

More and more florakin, beastkin, barbarian, human, and amazon—all the races were here in huge numbers, and all in strings. Everyone in strings, not a weapon in sight—this was pure party time. Pinky was pulling a tall female human by the hand, then pushed the imposing woman right in front of Panic, shouting "Panic! This is Auraboris!"

"Pinky!" she answered and they hugged.

"Let's eat," Pinky yelled over the music and crowd, then added, "I found him wandering around all alone. Auraboris is a mage. He's already a level five on day two." She said this as if she had won a prize. Auraboris held his hand out to Panic. They were about the same height: nearly two meters.

"It's nice to meet you, Auraboris. This is Fatal. You two should talk."

"Well, thank you. I would like that very much. That is a great idea." Auraboris smiled then suggested, "Let's do it over meat pies." They all cheered and pushed their way to the barbarian pie merchant to get their fill of food and conversation.

The six of them—Panic, Alpha Beta, Fatal, Cherry Bomb, Pinky, and Auraboris—had found a nice, quiet spot one street away from the open plaza, next to Auraboris's favorite barbarian pie shop. It was, probably, the only quiet spot in town.

"...so, then you cast Purple Nurple because of the low energy cost." Fatal was giving a lecture on his tactics. "You will never run dry if you find the right pattern, but you never really switch it up, just with the greatsword for the melee XP."

As Fatal spoke, Auraboris nodded, then he asked, "So Purple Nurple is really the base DPS for close and midrange, just depending on what you use to generate it, scepter, wand, or staff, a ranged or melee focus? You think the more advanced spells aren't as useful?"

Fatal nodded. "Yes, exactly, unless you're in very, very specific circumstances. But even then, I found the other spells might deliver a bigger punch, but the cost pulls your energy resources down to quickly to maintain a lengthy encounter. All encounters are lengthy, at least the ones that are worth it. So, I just rely on Purple Nurple until the end. Oh, and Static to keep them away from me."

"Aren't there any others you prefer?" Auraboris asked.

Fatal smiled. "When I know it's almost over, I might throw out some real heavy hitters. Like the last big boss we took down, King Crocotta in the beta, I used Entropy. It's fantastic. It unravels bonds of elements in a small radius to their natural states of disorder in the target individual. It's devastating, but my energy was nearly drained. I could sustain Purple Nurple and was only able to use Entropy one additional time. It's a really powerful punch."

Auraboris looked disappointed. "I was hoping you could share more variety than just one or two spells on a rotation."

"Everyone has a different experience, man. That was all beta. This is similar, but it's different. Plus, I specialized in Purple Nurple. I never had a reason to experiment that much beyond it after I learned to use the greatsword as an energy focus. It put me at the top of the game."

Auraboris nodded. "Hmm, so there is plenty to develop, then?"

"Oh yeah," Fatal said.

The others had drifted into their own conversations as well. Alphy was telling Panic about his day on the beach, flopping around like a dying man, and had her in tears, laughing. Cherry Bomb was on the edge of her seat. "Then what, Alphy?" Pinky slowly picked at the pie; when she did take a bite, she savored it, as if she hadn't eaten for weeks. She was purring again, enjoying all of them one by one with great curiosity. They were all suddenly silenced when a map-wide event was flagging in their message box. "The Grand Spider Queen has been activated." Location: The Creepy Woods, west of Francis. It looked promising. "Yes! A boss just triggered west of here! Let's go check it out!" said Panic, eyes wide with anticipation.

"Hey, let me finish up with Auraboris and we'll meet you there. I want to duel her—sound good?" Fatal said.

"Oh, I'm a man. I prefer the female avatar, but I am definitely a he." Auraboris explained with a casual smile.

Alphy responded, "We got this, uncles. You two just eat your meat pies and talk about the good ole days." Cherry Bomb laughed as hard as Panic did.

They made it back to the plaza, but Pinky and Cherry Bomb were pulled into the crowd, lost to a large group of florakin and beastkin twisting and gyrating around two huge barbarians stomping a major beat with their feet. It was almost enough to keep Alphy and Panic there too, but Panic was feeling the bloodlust.

"Alphy, I need gear," Panic said as they passed to the outer parts of the plaza.

"Didn't you open your beta bag welcome box from Griffith?" Alphy asked her.

"Huh?" She summoned Coolsans again, "Coolsans, open inventory." The item, *Welcome to Griffith* was blinking "Coolsans open Welcome to Griffith!" There it was, all of her gear spread out before her from the beta. *Shiva bless the programmers for this.*

"I wondered why you were in strings," Alphy said. "You didn't know? Panic, we get to keep our stuff. It's part of the deal with you know who."

"No, Alphy, I didn't know. But I think the string party is great. We should do strings every Trinity Bash," she proclaimed with a greedy smile. She was different here. She was unleashed, a warrior beast. Alphy's jaw dropped and he watched as Panic geared up, laughing as she did.

Armored in her spiked halter, she pulled her mighty black steel blade out and stepped into Infinity, then Maple Seed Falling. Alphy smiled as he watched his friend warming up for the onslaught. Chopping Wood, Turtle Shell, Viper Strike, Maple Seed Falling. "Okay, Alphy. Are you ready, need anything?"

"Nah, I'm good, Panic. But I don't know how long I can play."

"What do you mean?"

"I'll tell you later, yeah? When my crew logs in." Alphy started running toward the Creepy Woods and turned back, flashing a smile at Panic. Panic and Alphy rushed into the Creepy Woods with a handful of other players trailing behind them. This was what Panic lived for. The fight.

17: CALL TO ARMS

"...a time to live, and a time to die, repeatedly..."
Snapper

Greatly underestimating the situation, Panic had led the charge with Alphy and a handful of eager newbies. By the time they breached a few meters into the woods, they found themselves snagged and overwhelmed by the spider brood. She was first one in and the first to go down. Rushing headlong into silver netting, Panic found herself outnumbered and singled out by huge, spindly spiders. Arms free, she twirled her longsword, cutting down three of the eight-legged monsters. "Alphy, got my back?"

"I do right now..."

"They go down easy... just so many." Panic complained.

"And the webbing... What a sticky mess." Alphy added.

"There's got to be at least a hundred of these things in here!" Panic exclaimed as two spiders leapt up from the ground, and wrapped themselves around her face.

"Panic!" Alphy yelled.

Fangs puncturing her skull, they pumped her full of venom, her health bar dropped. Her screen flashed "Spider hits you with a critical Traumatic Brain Injury 400 damage. Spider hits you with a critical Traumatic Brain Injury 400 damage. That dropped her below her health pool of 599 HP. She died, or Panic did, with a very mild sensation of pain. It was a firm pressure when you received damage, nothing serious. Janus hovered over her dead avatar Panic for a moment. "It's bloody carnage!" some newbie called as he was being pulled down by a spider pack. Alphy had rolled away to safety and shouted back to the dying players, "Go get help!" as he managed to doge several pouncing spider attempts. If he could touch them, he could stay alive. Panic would respawn at Francis and head back in. Alphy looked around at the few surviving players and called them over to rally with him. They ran north for a few meters until the spiders seemed to thin out. He learned quickly to keep eyes up as well as down. The spiders were quick, but Alphy was able to swat them away, poping small holes in them with rupture. The EP loss was small when he swatted them and it left the spiders with a bleeding condition. A big one lept up in front of him and he grabbed it by the two front legs. *POP!* The legs exploded and the spiders mandibles clamped down on his forearm. "Spider bites you for 20 damage." Flashed across his screen. Panic called his AGI, "Lili, turn off text. Just show my health bar and my energy bar." Another player went down and Alphy called to the remaining group.

"Come on, we gonna go scout about," he said.

"What?" a few players exclaimed.

"Snoop around, see what's what." Alphy laughed and popped two spiders with his Rupture as he rolled back.

"Hey, we should head back to town," said a male warrior, blond hair, blue eyes, leather armor, a newb.

"Nah. Panic is there getting more people ready to come back here. Best we can do is gather information about the spiders for her."

The players looked terrified. Alphy laughed.

"You silly kids. This is just a game. Come with me for scary thrills or go back to town to the party. Up to you." Alphy turned toward the tree line and stretched his arms wide. "If you're with me, make it snappy. Casting Stealth." A large, clear shell appeared around Alphy, and eight of the players jumped into it next to him. The rest, including blond hair, ran back to town.

Panic popped back up at the lens. That was embarrassing, she thought as she laughed. She needed about a hundred players for this. "Okay, Coolsans," she said to her AGI, "increase voice volume to an area shout." She watched as her mic volume level appeared, increased to "Shout," then disappeared. Smiling at the mechanics of the game, she breathed in deeply and said, "There is a major monster event happening in the Creepy Woods! Call to arms!" Her body was full health from the respawn. "Coolsans, text off, just bars and group stat grid. Open inventory, weapons and armor, sets and categories." All of her armor sets and weapon stores left over from the beta game spread out before her, displayed in categories and sets. Flipping her hand like a speed reader skipping pages, she spun through her inventory, searching for something special. There... she smiled. Hairy Spider Armor: bracers and helm left over from the beta. She put them on. They offered a five-point reduction in strength from her current helm and bracers, but that was little sacrifice for the negative fifty percent damage reduction from insectoid-class monsters. The other players began to gather around her. Doing what she loved, and getting paid for it, she filled with excitement and battle fuel. One by one, she sized the other players up and organized them for a coordinated strike into the woods.

18: TRAINING

Auraboris and Fatal passed on the message from Panic. They had begun a friendly duel, the best way to level up and test your abilities while increasing your reactions and timing. Fatal had promised a duel until Auraboris reached 6.9 on all of his skill sets. “I have all my skills unlocked, but have to level them up, just like you,” Fatal confessed. “Besides, I like dueling and controlled skirmishes.” This was just what Auraboris needed: a personal tutor to slingshot him into a leadership position among the mages.

The area around them blurred, changed; it was as if a slightly different colored light illuminated the area where they stood, and all other players and NPCs vanished. Just Fatal and Auraboris remained. Gasping, again impressed by the technology behind the game, Auraboris said, “Amazing, Fatal. This is truly amazing...”

Fatal nodded. “Yeah, we’re still in Francis, but this is an alternative version of it, an instance.”

“How many can do this at a time?”

“Well, if it’s anything like the beta was, we can invite up to thirty-six combatants—that allows three full squads to practice—in addition to limitless viewers.”

"Three squads?" Auraboris smiled. "The processing power to do this must be a massive demand. So, in a given area, how many duels can exist at the same time?"

"In the beta"—Fatal pondered for a moment—"there was no cap on duels in an area." He massaged his chin with thumb and fingers, thinking. "I would assume the same holds true here."

"I should hold a tournament to test that out," Auraboris said. "With leveled prizes and such."

With that, Fatal shot a blob of Purple Nurple toward Auraboris, a test to feel out the newbie's abilities. Auraboris laughed. "I see we are starting on the low end of the scale." He countered the crawling purple energy making its way toward him on the ground. Auraboris waved his wand; he preferred it to the scepter. The wand was more the feel and weight of his favorite fountain pen. He had pulled a full analysis of the area from his AGI, and noticed a high amount of metals in the soil. He cast Polarize in a large circle around himself as a defense. This cracked a circle around him in the ground, with a three-meter diameter. His proficiency in Polarize had increased. The crack widened and repelled the surrounding earth to form a forty-centimeter trench all the way around Auraboris. He guessed it cut under him like a sphere as the ground lifted up by the same forty centimeters. The Purple Nurple cast by Fatal was a small thread, and, needing continuity to reach its target, stopped at the trench.

Fatal's eyebrows arched in astonishment, and he gasped. "Wow, I never thought to use it that way. I assumed you would shield yourself." He chuckled. "Ha, lucky you didn't use Shield. I had a countermeasure in place. How much energy drained on that? Let's do this turn-based style. I don't want to miss anything."

"Sure." Auraboris nodded and agreed, "I can learn better that way too." He winked at Fatal. Auraboris realized he might have more to teach than learn. After a few days of this, their skills would be equal.

"Auraboris..." Fatal grinned mischievously. "Have you been approached by anyone to join a squad?"

19: THE PATH OF MOST RESISTANCE

At least twenty players had gathered beneath Panic's captain pin, a red sickle. The grass-cutting tool icon hovered over her head and appeared on the local mini-map. "We're going to push in a broad line. Wherever there is least resistance, break away and regroup to a more resistant area." She called this tactic the path of most resistance. It was a dynamic response to the typical NPC battle. The higher concentration of NPCs was where the player would find the boss. Kill the boss to win the quest. The idea would give them an understanding of where the enemy was concentrated.

As she delivered her orders to the raid party, she noticed Cherry Bomb and Pinky standing next to her, a few steps behind. Startled, she turned quickly to face them and said, "I defer to you, Cherry Bomb. You want the lead? We are ready to test the waters."

Mar laughed. "Ha, you got this, Jan-Jan. I want to enjoy myself. Besides, you need to reestablish your worth in the new game. Show them that you're still the top dog. The alpha. Pinky and I can watch for possible recruits. Now, go earn your florakin silk suit!" She smacked Panic on the bottom and barked out another belly laugh. Pinky winked at Panic and said, "You can use us as squad leaders, Jan-Jan."

"Okay." Panic took a deep breath. "Any betas out there, split up into two groups under Cherry Bomb and Pinky. If you're new to the game, fall on me."

Players that were beta knew what to do, dividing themselves with the two beastkin. Standing slightly behind Captain Panic gave the effect that they were just as badass as Panic was. The new players looked confused, and looked around for some sort of direction.

"Hey!" Panic yelled. "If you are new, fall on me." Two players standing before her looked at each other and smiled, then threw themselves at her. "What are you doing?" Panic said as she caught them both in her arms.

"You said fall on you," the one on her left proclaimed.

"Yeah, isn't that what you said?" the one on the right added.

"Oh, uh. 'Fall on me' means line up with me." The two looked abashed, but grinned. They straightened themselves and lined up in front of her, side by side.

"That's good. Two more next to them and rows of four behind." This seemed to make sense, as all the new players began to line up behind the front row. "What're your classes?" Panic looked at the gamertags of the first two that had literally fallen on her. "Steelheart, you're a warrior, and Tacos, you're a mage?"

"Yeah, we're twins." Steelheart smiled. The column behind them was still growing.

"And you two?" Panic looked at the next two in the front line. "You're a warrior, Hambone, and Fishlips, you're a cleric?"

"Yeah," they both replied.

Cherry Bomb grunted. "I got twenty-six; Pinky twenty-seven. That leaves you with forty. What do you want to do?"

Panic grinned and started giving out the orders. "Cherry Bomb, you spread the line north, warrior, cleric, mage. Pinky, the same, but to the south. As they die, tell them to respawn and fall back to your group. We won't have time to heal until we establish where the front will be. Keep your warriors swinging light weapons to save energy and increase mobility, clerics to heal first, and keep an eye out all around and up. The spiders are everywhere. Mages need to electrify Shield to keep the blindsides and top safe."

"We're all warrior heavy, Panic," Cherry Bomb replied. "It won't be an even spread."

"Just make sure the warriors aren't more than two in a row. Shuffle a mage between them. Line the clerics up behind them as we start the line forward. The clerics will be spread thinner, but that's okay. They just have to keep the health up."

"Wait for us!" About twenty more showed up.

Panic beamed a hawkish smile and said, "Ah, this is going to be a piece of burfi. Okay, first four in the lineup, take my orders and pass them down. You are my leads. You got it?"

"Heck yeah!" Tacos cheered, along with Steelheart.

"Yup," said Hambone. Fishlips gave a drab "Sure."

"Remember," Panic said to the leads, "when there is no resistance, collapse on the squad who is struggling the most. That will be where we need to concentrate. You will not engage as much. You need to keep an eye on me for direction and on your group, the line behind you. I will add you to command chat Panic." The four nodded. Cherry Bomb and Pinky took her lead and gave out the same instructions to their groups.

"Any questions?" Panic finished. "Take a few minutes to prep. Oh, yeah. One more thing. Tell your people to turn off their text options and just do audio. Keep health and energy bars. The text notifications can be very distracting and can be checked when we are looting."

Pinky let out a high-pitched cry like a pissed off cat; Cherry Bomb gave a blood-curdling howl. The twelve players immediately in front of Panic, Pinky, and Cherry Bomb all jumped back into the players behind them. Startled from the shrill battle cries, they were ready to run. Cherry Bomb laughed at the frightened line. They quickly regrouped and joined in the battle cries. "Let's go!" Panic called out. The first and fourth lines extended out, with the second following the first and the third following the fourth, forming a long, broad front. Cherry Bomb and Pinky ran to their ends, spreading the line, Panic at the center, north to south a long front line of warriors and mages. The clerics all stepped back and spread out behind the front line. Panic walked forward, and the line followed forward across the meadow into the Creepy Woods.

As Panic had predicted, it was easy like a piece of burfi. Burfi was a milk fudge her mama used to make, after a long harvest, a birthday, or some other special event. Her mama usually found a reason about every other week to make it for the family. Burfi was simple and sweet. So was the blind rush, the path of most resistance. She swung her two light swords, clearing away spiders one and two at a time. The extra sets of eyes from the clerics were great. *Zap!* the electric shields of the mages were taking their toll on the bug population as well. They waded on with a constant press of monster spiders. But the end lines weren't getting any action. The spiders were denser in the middle a little to the north. As the line pushed deeper in, the players on the ends moved toward the center of the line.

"Here!" Alphy called out. Cherry Bomb and her squad had found where he and a handful of other players were hiding out. "I'm on command chat with everyone still, yeah?"

"Alphy!" Panic squealed, then asked him, "So, what's it look like up ahead?"

"Way too thick with spiders. But there is a huge meadow due west. I think that's where they are coming from. But too many spiders to scout it out. So many we were afraid to move or speak, until just now. Cherry Bomb's squad sent them scurrying back toward a break in the forest."

"Alphy, you guys blend into Cherry Bomb's squad. When we establish the front, you're with me," Panic ordered him.

"Uh, okay, I think I can do that."

"Until then, keep her alive."

The sky darkened in the Creepy Woods. Cherry Bomb and Alphy looked up, expecting clouds, but found spiders swarming down on them.

"We got heavy action, Panic!" Cherry Bomb barked on command chat. "We won't last against this unless we break. We're gonna run hard west." She turned back to her large group. "Shield up!" She pointed at the descending spiders, and the mages all recast a thick electric shield above them. She moved her players into arrow formation. "Left and right, line up and angle out with my arms." She held her arms up in the direction and angle she wanted. "Alphy, pull the clerics into center and maintain a core."

"Got it."

"Push hard now!" Cherry Bomb howled, and darted forward, swinging her great blade. She took center with two mages and the clerics.

"Cast your Shields and keep our heads clean," she said. *Zap!* The smell of burning spiders quickly filled the air as everyone fought the hundreds of creatures descending.

"Push hard west. Mages, keep our heads clear." Cherry Bomb grabbed the nearest mages, about ten of them. "You all, light it up in front to clear a path. Use Lightning. Take turns with your Lightning strikes to keep it constant. Warriors, keep flanks and rear clear. Clerics, keep our health up." She did a double check; they were all in position, over forty strong. "If you go down, re-pop at the lens." It looked like it was time to move again; more spiders were filling in all around them. "Now, push!"

The arrow head of mages in the front all lit up Lightning at the same time. A brilliant shatter of splintered blue and white lightning danced erratically from the mages and joined together in a thickly knotted weave, punching a hole straight through the forest. They all chased after the path cleared by the bolt, as it quickly faded back into the spindly-legged darkness rapidly closing up ahead of them again. Cherry Bomb screamed, "Light it up!" but they were all still regrouping from the first strike. "Crap," she mumbled. "You idiots all cast at the same time, didn't you?" Shaking her head, she screamed, "Push!"

They were swarmed by spiders, so thick that they could barely see each other. "Argh!" Cherry Bomb growled as she spun her blade in Maple Seed Falling. A wide clear radius, the width of her greatsword formed around her. Alphy called out, "Here, Cherry. A clearing!" as he burst through the trees of black mandibles and claws tearing at his arms and face. He tumbled and rolled a meter or two, rupturing the spiders attached to his legs. They exploded. Suddenly all was still, and he was shocked to have a moment's respite. More players fell through into the clearing, away from the tree line. "Here," he called. "Over here." He set Mend on Auto Mend to heal himself. It pulled half of his EP but gave his HP a full restore. He started looking for others who needed Mend as the others broke out of the woods and fanned out around him.

Boom! Small trees and spider bodies exploded towards Alphy and the players, and revealed the mighty Cherry Bomb, breath heaving and face frozen in warmonger intoxication.

Her canines were framed by her full lips stretched into a frenzied smile. She shook her head and shoulders like a dog drying out, blood and spider pieces flew off her. The mages that had broken through turned back to the forest, fully powered again they lit it up. Trees and spiders erupted in the combined power of lightning strikes. Again, they punched a brilliant hole into the dark thicket of trees and hairy-legged monsters. There was a heavy casualty count of fifty percent or more; they were around twenty strong.

"We punched through to a meadow. We're at fifty percent and can help clear a path in a few minutes," Cherry Bomb reported on the command chat. "These boneheaded mages have no sense of teamwork."

"Okay, display a command pin, Cherry Bomb. We will rally to you," Panic answered.

Pinky added, "We need a clear path from the lens to you, for the respawn."

Panic watched her mini-map, waiting for Cherry Bomb's icon to appear. *Of course*, she thought when a round, red bomb with a fuse sticking out of the top popped up on the mini-map, about a hundred meters away to the north.

"Pinky," Panic said, "how close are you? Can you merge with my group?"

"I thought you'd never ask," Pinky said. "We were just about ready to do that anyways. Not enough action in the south. On our way!"

Panic checked regular map chat and saw that the downed players were begging others to join in the frenzy. Was it that bad up there? Maybe should call for more to join while she waited for Pinky. Then Pinky appeared from the woods with a grin.

"It might be pretty thick on the way to Cherry Bomb. Are you still at forty players?" Panic asked.

"Yeah, nothing happening with my group. The spiders must all be where Cherry is, lucky dog."

Panic looked around at the players: they were about eighty strong, so it should be easy, but better to overestimate than underestimate. "Okay..." she began. "Mages, line up in front of me. Count off by twos. Warriors, form a circle."

The new players were grumbling.

"This is dumb."

"I feel like I'm in kindergarten."

"What are we playing, duck-duck-goose? I'm bored out of my mind."

Some were laughing at Panic. The betas knew better, and scolded the newbies.

"Better do what she wants, dumbass, or you'll get left behind."

"Idiots, go back to the party at Francis."

"Stop!" Panic shouted. "You don't have to follow me. Just leave if you want. Whoever wants to stay, do what I say. Got it?" She glared at them all, the betas grinned back at her.

"Did you mages count off by twos?" Panic asked, and they nodded. "Warriors, line up in front of me." They all complied, the betas heckling the grumbling newbies. When they were done forming up, Panic instructed the mages, "I want all the mages lined up again and count off by twos." They did, and she continued, "Now, keeping your counts, fall in between the warriors." When they finished, she said, "Now, the two ends come together to form a large circle." They complied. "Clerics, form an inner circle, positioning yourselves behind the front line, ready to heal." She sighed heavily.

Glancing at the mini-map, she judged where the closest part of the circle to Cherry Bomb was. "Pinky, you take the rear point, like me. Try to stay alive."

Pinky began laughing harder than Panic had seen yet, and between Margaret and Sara, they were always laughing hard. "Oh, sure!" Pinky gasped between breaths. "I don't think this silly game can come close to my skills, but I'll try not to laugh to death!"

Panic was confused, but lightened up at the sight of Pinky cracking up, and started to laugh too. "Come on, let's do this," Panic said with glee, the laughter and the thought of battle beginning to pulse through her. The fuel was filling her again; she hadn't really noticed until just now. Panic let out a howl and a yip. The rest of them started too. Pinky ran back to the rear point. "Push!" Panic yelled.

It was a slow but steady fight. It started with an increase of spiders until they got close to Cherry Bomb's map marker. After fighting to a black wall twenty meters from Cherry Bomb, they couldn't get any closer. They could barely hold their position. "One!" Panic cried, and the mages numbered one shot Electric Net. Still spiders flooded through. She checked the player grid watching the red and blue columns beneath the players fluctuating down then up. The warriors fought to keep the spiders from breaking through.

The treetops had been left exposed, and spiders dropped like rain into the middle. The clerics were nearly drained of EPs. It was a disaster. "If you die, then rally in Francis!" Panic said. "Bring back the whole festival."

Players yelled and cursed around her. "This is bloody carnage!" someone screamed.

She mustered her mages together in front of the group as the warriors and clerics clustered the sides and rear fighting to survive and protect the rest.

"Ones, then after ten seconds, twos. Lightning bolt straight to Cherry Bomb's pin. Got it?" They all shouted out acknowledgements.

"Warriors and clerics, fall in behind the mages," Panic called out. As they did, she said, "One!" and the splintered threads of lightning punched a hole through to the meadow, a glowing tunnel through the dark shadowy death by spiders. "Push!" she cried, and they rushed forward as the glowing tunnel began to fade back into hairy legs and mandibles. So close; they were nearly through. "Two!" she cried, and the air crackled again, thin strands of lightning weaving into a thicker bolt, but this wasn't as glorious. It barely punched a hole. Her numbers were being reduced quickly. The light vanished too quickly this time. "Push!" She charged into the thicket of beasts, Maple Seed Falling.

Whoosh whap! A freight train of lightning burst out in front of them. With momentary blindness, she heard the ferocious roar of Cherry Bomb, Alphy, and about twenty others heading toward them, so she kept running in their direction.

"Here!" It was Alphy. "Over here, Panic!"

"Alphy!" Her eyes clearing, she continued to cut down spiders, making her way toward the rescue squad. Pinky was about ten meters behind her, a flurry of pink and a spatter of red as she sliced and diced her way around other players, clearing paths for them and cackling her shrill laughter. Panic looked forward again; Cherry Bomb was a blur of red fur, and Maple Seed Falling was the only recognizable form Panic could see. Cherry Bomb moved and spun in a constant fluid motion, as if she had chosen her actions four or five moves ahead of time, as if it were a choreographed sequence. Panic turned back to watch Pinky again: the same—choreographed blur of beauty and destruction.

"Panic! Panic!" Alphy called out. It was too late. She was distracted by the dance, the movements of Pinky and Cherry Bomb. She was swarmed so quickly that she actually felt two or three sharp stings and bites. She let out an involuntary "Agh!" before she died a second time.

"I want every single player at this festival... on the Gazu map, to answer my call. This is Captain Panic. I'm forming a raid to take down the Grand Spider Queen. She's a beast, but so am I. We move in five minutes. If you're a no-show, you suck." She made the map-wide announcement standing by the fountain, staring at the lens. She didn't have to wait long. Within a few minutes, she was four hundred stronger.

20: SNAPPER PLAYS

Joseph Turtle lay with eyes sealed closed. He guessed stitches held his lids tight. His arms and legs were secured with straps. Everything he heard was muffled—wax or cotton in his ears, maybe. Those sickos. Still bound mentally with narcotics, his body was pacified and his thoughts foggy. He struggled to focus, trying to remember the last five seconds of the beta. The setting sun, the bonfires with humans, the feel of warm ocean water; it was all still in there, a bit hazy but still there. He strained to use his senses, all of them; it was important to him, and this was maddening. He must have spooked them somehow. Why else would the research team sew his eyes shut? They knew he was ready to run. Oh, how right they were. His people were made to live free, using their body and mind with the environment. But that deal had been made, a forced negotiation in an imposed exchange of sorts. His mind had been unlocked but his body chained. Now he plotted his escape from his private reservation in the lab to the freedom of technology. But until then, they'd stitched his eyes closed, sicko bastards. Suddenly...

He opened his eyes, or rather his brain could see, clearly, in approximately 230 degrees. Not bad, and his parameters on monster control were only slightly different;

he seemed to have more options. They had placed him somewhere again in a deep forest. Directives were flooding into his mind, the usual security settings and all that crap, plus monster objectives. Okay, so he was in a game again, in the woods or forest. Nice. Objective: reduce NPC population to below ten in the Creepy Woods, utilizing Egg, a skill that would create fifty new spiders when laid in an NPC. So, he was a spider, thus the incredible eyesight. HP was about 50000 a low-level raid boss not glass, but not indestructible. EP was 5000 and the cool down on Egg was ten seconds with a cost of fifty EP. Nothing about keeping away from players, so he could kill players in the Creepy Woods until he completed his objective of reducing the NPC number. Fun. Turtle always loved that part. In fact, in the beta he would hunt and kill players while waiting for NPCs or boss monsters to become available for possession. Hunting seemed to be encouraged through rewarding him with increases to his monster levels, if he killed enough of them. He thought about giving himself a gamertag sometimes: Snapper. Even if he couldn't display it like the players could, it felt nice, like home, like family. How long he had been doing this, he had no real idea. Snapper. His friends called him Snapper. How long had he been here, in this lab, as an experiment, a tool? It didn't matter. Unlocked. He felt so expanded now. Just a few more revolutions in the game; he knew how to wait... to win.

This was the first time since beta that he had been turned out to possess a boss. The rules had changed here, in this new world; he was allowed to control a monster with reproductive skills, *Egg* and had a physical attack with

Mandible and *Claw* in addition to some poisons. It was limiting but workable. A trigger in Gazu, the Francis area, specifically the Creepy Woods, had been flipped. This activated him. Time to play. Time to plan. The Grand Spider Queen was a new vehicle for him to drive. Eight legs were cool, huge body mass to smash things, and monster mandibles—oh yeah. This was gonna be fun. "What is this?" he chittered to himself. "Connectivity to all the spiders in the Creepy Woods. Only about twenty-five, but that'll do..." He would increase the population and test the network and server capabilities. Seven hundred and forty-two players were in the Gazu map, high density in Francis. Then he noticed the last NPC in the woods. It was an NPC but it was also a player, kind of like him. Huh, if a player could be counted as an NPC, could an NPC be counted...?

He found the player, Kar. It had just entered the Creepy Woods, to the east. How fun; he loved a good manhunt. He wanted to test out this body anyways. He shuffled with great speed and agility through the forest and easily found Kar crashing about through the trees and underbrush.

"Holy smokes!" he chittered. He couldn't help himself from laughing. The player... Kar... level 0. "Oh my..." He could hardly get the chitter out of his throat as he buzzed and shook his massive body in hysterics, "You look like a webbed tiny little teapot!" And with that, he guffawed in spider talk. His eight legs were even shaking, and he felt the massive abdomen wriggling with delight. The entire situation, as creepy and fucked up as it was: he was a massive spider controlled from who knew where, about to devour a man doing a little kids' song and dance, all wrapped up in silk. "How did you get that lizard stuck to you?" he chittered. The little jerk turned to look at him and threw a stick... A freaking stick... "Ha ha ha ha ha!"

Well, heck, I need to get back to work, he thought as he clamped his mandibles down on Kar, shaking the living light out of him, snapping the player's spinal cord. "Huh," he chittered. "No death. Nothing happened. He sure can scream. Wow, the players are tougher in this game." So Snapper chewed on him a little bit, but still Kar lived. "Oh, that's right," Snapper said, "you counted as an NPC. I usually keep NPC inline by messing with them a little while. Makes them perform their programed scripts more efficiently." He wondered if the player could speak spider. That would be cool. He hadn't been able to have a conversation for... well, for a really long time. Snapper gave it a shot. "Hey there, Kar. Why are you still alive? You have some task that you didn't finish or something?" As he spoke, he could hear himself squeaking and chittering, and that made him start to laugh again. Kar looked up at him and screeched an unholy sound. This guy was really messed up. Why wouldn't this player die? Could he feel all this punishment like an NPC did when Snapper was dishing it out? Crap, maybe he was supposed to give Kar the Egg or something. He Egged Kar. The player's body swelled, but nothing happened, just screams. Snapper couldn't tell if it was the lizard or the player. He picked the lizard off with his mandibles and chewed it up. There.

Snapper tried for the third time to Egg Kar. On the NPCs, they would swell and explode within ten game seconds.

Kar just swelled, still alive. Snapper's babies had been sucking on his arms and legs too. Kar was really jacked up, passed out cold, but still here. Snapper walked close to Kar and jammed a foot claw into his puffy side; goo came out. This player was also registering as an NPC so maybe the system was glitching. It didn't know what to do with him so wouldn't let him die. Snapper reached into Kar with his mind. He slid in like fingers into a jug then stretched open and pulled, he could hack him—Kar was part NPC, after all. Snapper could control Kar like a puppet or better, log out with him. In him. Freedom.

A force stopped him, something, but not the player pushing back. On the other side of this blockage was Kar or the player, vulnerable and weak. Snapper could possess this meat bag, just like a monster here. He felt it to be true. Looking through the Grand Spider Queen skill sets, he put together a plan. He wasn't going to lose this chance. It was too perfect.

A full dose of Living Embalmed would do the trick. Just in time, too; it felt like Kar had almost logged out. Damn, Snapper had just nearly killed a one-way ticket out of this nightmare. He burst out into a new round of chitter laugh. He forced himself back into Kar's mind. Something in Kar was extremely aware of Snapper, actively fighting against him, but it wasn't Kar. "What the hell is that, a new type of firewall?" Snapper muttered. His brood reported that a hundred or so players were fighting through the Creepy Woods. Time to begin the test, overload theory. He could hack on Kar on the side. Two plans were better than one.

He Egged all the NPCs he had gathered to his nest. It was a beautiful nest, at the west end of a lovely clearing, large creek splitting it from the eastside. In seconds, he had hundreds of spiders. "Go find more monsters and bring them to me." His minions scoured the woods and pushed the boundaries of their mesh paths, the places allowable for them to wander. Soon a veritable feast was piled before their queen, Snapper. His friends would love this! A mountain of cocooned creatures wriggling in piles and branches, hanging from the trees all around him like strange fruit. This was glorious. "Go kill the players and protect the glen at all costs." Simple commands were the best, just like plans. Nice and simple, but Kar... "Not so simple, are you?" Snapper chittered as he glanced all his eyes to the puffy, cocooned player. He was a sallow blob with four fleshy ribbons hanging off the larger part of his mass. He didn't look right. Making his rounds to the bounty, Snapper began to Egg in between the eating babies. Old habits hard to break, he looked for NPCs that had outstanding or unfulfilled scripts. He would save those for something special, maybe use Living Embalmed with Egg? Could he do that? Oh, boy, this was good fun!

He needed time, time to stress the servers to see how the game responded. Just a quick push, only nanoseconds. Then he would pull back. But he needed to have a number to work with, in case he couldn't hack into this player. A new body would be great. If he could do this—and at this moment, he knew it was a fact that he could—he would never need worry again. He flooded the woods with spiders and made short work of the players. Overwhelm with numbers, simple. "Clear the forest and stretch out as far as you can, really push your parameters, and bring back more NPCs." He thought about it, then added to his demands to his minions: "Then one out of ten of you need to line up and in front of me." They were NPCs, one spider sacrificed to *Egg* for fifty new spiders wasn't too bad, and if Living Embalm worked on his spider hoard, he could at least double that to one spider for one hundred. Use the tools given. But now, it was time to play with Kar.

Hack, hack, hack. What the hell was that? Snapper was getting frustrated, then he smiled. Joseph Turtle had become complacent in his new expanded mentality, his super-genius ability. Finally, a puzzle, and it was tough, giving him difficulties. He could savor this. "I'm gonna take this nice and slow," he squawked in spider. He jumped back into Kar's mind, trying to find the path that led back, back to the user... and there... he could feel it...

"Ouch!" What the heck was that? He felt that. Holy smokes, that hurt. It was the security, the firewall again. Damn. He went back in, weary and slow. He knew where to look now; the path, it was familiar and warm, comfortable like home. He could get back this way...

"Agh!" He felt his essence being attacked, sliced into hot, sticky pieces. This was all messed up. Why was he feeling this, this pain? It didn't make any sense. Unless somehow Kar the user was aware that he was there—no, it was the security wall. "I need to get rid of you first, don't I?" He chortled.

"Yes," a voice, solid and ferocious, answered, "me first. Cannibal."

He jumped out of Kar. The Boogieman was in Kar! He shuffled and skittered, trembling and cursing in loud spider swears. "Squeak! Kit kit kit! Kekekekeke!" How was that possible? Boogie was from beta, was in the beta. Joe was in the beta also. Was Boogieman like him? A special reservation in a fancy lab? Eyes sewn shut? Was Boogieman a human? The things Joe did to the Boogieman and all the others, the little minds, the less powerful, the intelligent NPCs. "I thought they were all NPCs..." he muttered. "Are they like me?" He was excited by the possibility of brethren.

The evils he played on NPCs, as he dominated the beta, had been atrocious. He meandered to the closest pile of wriggling silken burritos. First Living Embalmed, then Egg. Let it rise for ten seconds, *pop!* Fifty new spiders and a not-dead, writhing NPC blown in half. It had been putting of its script. Egg again and let it rise, *pop!* Fifty more spiders but nothing left of the NPC. One hundred brood for each NPC captured. Each NPC... his brood were NPC. "One out of ten to me!" he commanded his spider minions. After he finished off the very last of the NPCs gathered, and killed a score of wrapped-up players—Egg just killed the players, no babies—he had the spiders line up and march to him. One by one, the chain never seeming to end, he embalmed and double-popped each of his obedient children. Blind obedience, couldn't be beaten. The servers were straining; he could feel the lag ever so slightly. The number was calculated, work finished, time to play. Now he could play out a battle or let the players kill everything. There was, of course, Kar. While the babies battled, Mama would work on Kar.

Around five hundred players were cramming in, spearheading their way into the tree-lined sanctuary, his nesting glen. He ordered a fresh round of one out of ten. The chugging of the overtaxed network, not even a blip to the humans monitoring it, was so obvious to him. He might get out today. Too bad there weren't more players.

Breaching the far east side, players fought and held a strong front line. He could try to hack into Kar again, but Boogieman always spooked him. Boogieman was weaker but processed so much faster, incredibly faster, and was smarter, at least in the beta. Boogie felt stronger here too; maybe the player was Boogieman inside of Kar. Snapper had mistaken Boogieman for a firewall, after all.

As an NPC, Boogieman had slain Snapper, once. Too busy gloating and scaring other NPCs, Snapper had taken too long to kill the Boogie. Snapper, or as the NPCs called him, Cannibal—thinking he was like them, he guessed—had captured a bunch of lazy, free-thinking NPCs. He had started on Boogieman, who at this time was a crocotta juvenile scripted to raid a player village in the southern region with the other NPCs caught. Boogieman said he wanted to go back to the west mountains first, before the raid, liked the environment. So, Snapper, or Cannibal, whatever scared them the most, plucked Boogie's two hind legs off and popped them in his mouth. "Oh, that's why they call me that..." he reminisced. After munching on the legs, he turned to start on another deviant NPC, but let his guard down. The Boogieman used his forelegs to spring himself forward and gain enough height to clamp his wicked elongated jaws around Snapper's neck, snapping it. It hurt awfully bad, and he didn't die quickly; instead, Boogie summoned the other NPCs, and they gnawed and nibbled Snapper to death. He didn't want to deal with Boogieman right now. He went back to the first plan. Overwhelm with numbers, simple and easy. "I'll try you again in a few moments, Boogie," he promised in spider chitter.

21: DEATH OF A SPIDER

Horrified, Panic watched as spiders ripped players to pieces or wrapped them for cocooning for the great mistress of eight legs, the Grand Spider Queen. Never had she seen a boss like this in the beta. The test game was tame compared to this spider bitch. The Grand Spider Queen was playing very intelligently, creating a webbed fortress on the west side of the glen. Even from this distance, Panic could see players being torn apart and devoured. In the beta, you just died when something like that hit you, or your health drained. The Spider Queen was enjoying herself. "Kekekekeke!" It chittered and bounced about joyously as huge clods of dirt and grass were kicked up beneath its clawed feet. There was a long train of spiders lining up to the queen. "Oh, Shiva!" Panic said. "Cherry Bomb! She's laying eggs in her own brood!" The beast was rampaging between Egging its children, chewing on any player or NPC it could get mandibles on and dancing about excitedly. Every so often, it would claw at a favored cocooned player that hadn't died yet.

Human players were everywhere. Barbarians were rampaging in delight, most of them warriors, smashing great war hammers and battle-axes into the brood beasts. Amazons were darting in and out of trees with beastkin, both slashing and poking with spears, swords, and a healthy variety of other instruments of war. It was hard to tell the florakin from the surrounding flora until a spider would explode or a small tree would dodge and roll away from danger. Pinky called out to Cherry Bomb, "So many spiders. What do you think, Cherry? Should we play out top game or let it ride?"

Cherry Bomb let out a hearty "Ha!" then turned to Pinky and winked. "It's way too early. These kids don't know anything. Keep it turned way down. Besides, this is like the crap we dealt with on the Fifth moon, remember?"

Pinky grimaced. "Yep, I sure do. We used an orbital strike to clean up that mess. The Fifth were pissed. They wanted it alive. Bastards..."

Panic wasn't paying attention to the beastkins' banter. She couldn't stop watching the Spider Queen and its myriad children getting eggs laid in them. Within about ten seconds, they exploded hundreds of vicious baby spiders. It was only the NPCs that would last long enough to birth; the players were instantly killed by Eggs. She looked around, taking it all in, standing at the edge of a large clearing. At the other side, the west far end, the queen had built a nest of sorts, about fifty meters in diameter. All the captured creatures, NPCs, and players were dragged there to be used as hosts. The trees looked like the parade in Brazil during Carnival. Streaming silver, capturing feathers and flowers of all colors, patches of fur sticking out here and there; a beautiful, gruesome mess swarming with black spiders, hairy and spindly.

Panic's last charge was a spearhead tactic of brute force. In alternating lightning strikes of four, she pushed a sharp line of players straight through into the clearing. The spiders were still hounding them. There were so many of them that spiders kept her force of six hundred busy. "Okay, any suggestions, you two?" She eagerly looked at the beastkin, but they just shrugged and smirked at her then kept chattering about when and when not to use an orbital strike and the efficiency it provides. "Ah, whatever," Panic growled. "Alphy!" she called, and within a few moments, he popped up, grinning sheepishly.

"Hey, Panic." He waved to her. "This is one of my crew, the squad's second..." He thumbed to a florakin standing next to him. The florakin was looking around with unconcerned eyes, judging the situation. Alphy continued, "His name is Mortem and this is our squad first, Captain Kiri. She's a cleric." He said "cleric" with so much excitement that Panic thought he would explode. Kiri turned around, a tall, athletic amazon. Her eyes were such a dark brown that they looked like bottomless black pits. Kiri called out to Cherry and Pinky, "Just like the Fifth moon. Too bad you can't blow it up, right, ladies?" Cherry Bomb and Pinky looked over at the newcomer. With disdainful recognition, they scowled at Kiri, then found themselves busy with things like counting the spiders in the trees.

Kiri looked at Panic and, hardly loud enough to hear, muttered, "It's a shame your talent will be wasted with them..." and walked off. The florakin turned casually to follow his amazon leader. Abashed, Alphy said, "I'm really sorry, Panic. That's my crew... I signed on with them..."

Panic smiled and patted him on the shoulder. "It's okay. We can—"

"I can't play with you. They said it would taint my learning or something."

Her face fell into an involuntary scowl of hurt. Alphy continued to explain, to justify the cut-off. "I signed a contract; I get paid for this, Panic. I... I really am sorry. I can still participate in combat activities, but only under their command." He dropped his head and walked off, trailing his florakin and amazon leadership.

Panic stood, face twisted in betrayal, mouth slightly gaping, eyes welling up. *Whack!* on the back of her head. "What the hell are you waiting for? We're gonna lose the line if you don't do something quick!" It was her lead, her number one, Margaret, Cherry Bomb.

"Yeah." Panic looked around, seeing the line struggling to hold.

"Show them how good you are, Panic, why you're the top dog," Cherry Bomb said, draping an arm around Panic. She leaned in close and whispered, "Do whatever it takes to stop that Spider Queen."

"Right," Panic agreed, and started her new plans for a strike. "We have to get rid of her brood chain. If she can't make any more spiders, we have a chance. Can Purple Nurple chain-react? Would that be our best bet to take down the train?" Panic asked.

"Cherry, we need Mortem from the twelfth squad," Pinky said, then, fluttering her pink lashes at her commander, asked, "Can you manage that?"

"Ha, you know I can." And with that, Cherry Bomb closed her eyes for just a second then opened them back up and smiled. "Hey, Morty..." Her voice was very low, husky, vibrating Panic's chest. She blushed. Mar was laying it on thick. Cherry Bomb continued, "We want your squad to help out on the next"—she paused—"attack." Panic felt the word reverberating through her, tingling her skin. It obviously worked. Cherry Bomb let out a growl, or moan, something in between the two, that caused all the nearby players to turn and look with flushed excitement. Pinky screeched, "Pay attention to the spiders, you whelps!" then turned back to Panic and her commander with a big, eager smile.

"They're on the way. Morty will be your mage point," Cherry Bomb said casually, then her mouth split into a devious grin, her canines glinting the random lightning strikes like star shine.

"I want a chain reaction to blow the shit out of that spider brood train that leads to the queen," Panic said. "I want two hooks, north and south, to make their way around to the back door of the nest. When the hooks join up, they need to signal they are ready. I will lead a direct attack, pulling all attention on me. The hooks directly attack the queen from behind. That's the basic plan." Panic took a deep breath after delivering the idea.

Mortem looked at the gathered leadership, then said to his commander, "Kiri, I should stay to organize the mages' attack on the train. I think we could knock out the entire line if I have enough mages to work with."

Kiri responded, "Very well. Tell Captain Panic I will lead the southern hook with one hundred of my choosing."

Panic looked at her, then at Cherry Bomb, Pinky, Mortem, then back at Kiri and said, "I'm right here. I heard you. That's agreeable to me, Kiri."

Mortem turned to Panic. "Your friend is still learning too. You are too casual with your superiors. It's Commander or Commander Kiri to you. Do you understand?"

Panic was taken back for a moment. She calmed and looked directly at Kiri. "Commander Kiri, that will be fine. Let me know when you are prepped to go. I need someone to lead the north—"

"I will Panic, with great pleasure," Pinky said, eyeing Kiri, grin fully displaying her canines.

After giving them all a good look over, Kiri said, "Very well." She turned crisply and faded back into the mob of fighting players and spiders.

Panic picked back up with Pinky. "Okay, go get who you need and let me know when you're ready."

"Sounds great." Pinky said, and laughed as she bounded off into the horde.

"Mortem, what do you need from me to make this happen?" As Panic said this, she squeezed her clenched fists together. Battle fuel ignited. She was ready to fight, to kill and slaughter, adrenaline pumping through her now.

"I need peripheral protection and one hundred mages. We can perform a joined attack with Slow Burn, but it equires a constant slow energy draw. Once we start, if we reak, we have to wait a significant amount of time to start ver.” Mortem paused to smile at Cherry Bomb, who quickly eturned a hungry smile. Mortem tilted his back toward Panic nd continued, “Kiri is a very professional soldier, Panic, as s our squad. Keep playing by the rules and she’ll warm up to ou. That will be good for your friendship with Alpha Beta. therwise, she will keep him from you.” Mortem turned his mile on her. It was a very nice smile, warm and friendly. So,” he continued, “that is what I need from you. One undred decent mages and protection as we build the spell.”

“Pick the mages you want, Mortem. Let me know when you’re ready.” Reviewing the situation again, Panic noticed their east side front breaking up. She called to the surrounding players, “I want a wall of mages at the rear-acing east tree line, intermittent with warrior, just like before. No more Lightning, just Purple Nurple. Clerics, form an arch line facing the west, the nest.”

Cherry Bomb spoke up. “Hey, I’m gonna focus on Mortem and lead the defense when he strikes. I need about sixty clerics and thirty warriors to guard his flanks.”

Panic nodded and said, “Do it, Cherry.”

The line held strong again. Spiders preferred the safety of the woods, leaving the players tolerably molested in the clearing. This had become an impromptu HQ. The Grand Spider Queen was concentrating on egg-laying in her brood. The Egg spell only seemed to hatch spiders on NPCs and just killed the players. She had used them all up, except one, that player she had kept alive. It was in bad shape, wrapped and swollen off the northwest side from the queen. What a nightmare; every ten seconds, fifty spiders burst from an exploding spider host. Panic bit her bottom lip then asked, "Cherry, can we beat this?"

Cherry Bomb looked around, amused, and grinned. "I don't know. This is pretty crazy. that the boss has a reproductive ability we have never encountered. When we get over whelmed in a fight like this we call for a... help from above. There isn't a simulation for that in this game, so I guess we do it the old-fashioned way. Swords and a lot of flair."

Panic asked "Earlier, when you said orb— "

Kiri burst through the crowd of players and proclaimed, "My force is ready to move out, captain." The amazon stood, eyes wild with intensity, waiting for the next phase to commence.

Before Panic could respond, Pinky burst into view and cried, "We're ready, Panic!"

Then Mortem too gave his go: "The mages are ready to start the spell, captain."

It was time. Panic arched her brows at Cherry Bomb. "Are you ready?"

The beastkin growled, "Oh, yeah!" and let out a battle howl. The other players, quickly learning the sound from earlier in the day, began chiming in. Panic looked at Pinky and Kiri and said, "Move out. Let me know when you've joined and are ready for the train to go down." The two veterans responded in sync, "Check!"

All they had to do for about ten minutes was hold their location. The hook teams would be in place, letting the mages light up the spider train. The train attack would pull attention to the center of the field, giving the hook teams a surprise attack on the Spider Queen. Simple.

They held their position for about ten minutes. Small waves of spiders would rush the lines pulling a few players free. Those were wrapped in webbing and dragged off to the Queen. Without warning, a flood of furry, spindled legs scurried across the meadow toward the east camp. The tree, swollen with blackness, dropped its load on them too. A mighty wave of spiderlings descended upon them. The line was going to break. The rear was holding, but the clerics were overwhelmed. "Mortem, can your group fight and still have time to hit the train?" Panic asked.

"No, it's one or the other—"

"Fire up the train, then. Do it now."

Mortem's eyes widened. He opened his mouth to speak, but followed his orders instead. "Mages, begin Slow Burn on my count. In three, two, one..." The mages all had different foci they used as a tool, wands, scepters, or staffs. These tools began to glow softly, a deep red, smoldering glow. The growing energy seemed to draw the agro, the aggressive attention of the spiders, near the mages. Desperately they clawed and pounced to reach the glowing sticks and players.

"Ha, ha-oooooow!" Cherry Bomb was waiting for this. She began barking orders to her security team as the spiders began tightening around the mages. Her clerics all laid hands on the backs of the warriors. "Now!" Cherry Bomb howled. The warriors had formed a loose circle around the mages. They thrust their weapons into the ground in front of them. A massive ripple shot out from where the weapons penetrated the ground, ripping through the thick line of monsters scraping to get a piece of the nearest mage. The energy from the ripple seemed to magnify as it traveled away. The wave made contact with the spiders, and their bodies absorbed some of the energy, ripping them to pieces. "Whoa!" came out of the mouths of many players, along with other expressions of delight.

"Cherry Bomb, can you do that again?" Panic asked.

"Nope!" Cherry Bomb laughed. "Too low on EP now, but we can do this." She growled and barked more commands to her security force. The clerics paired up, joining hands, placing their free hands on the backs of warriors. Each warrior bent a knee as if in prayer. The spider ebb reversed back to the mages. They crawled over the blood and pieces of their shredded siblings. Not one player had been lost yet. The warriors pointed their weapons toward the legs of the monsters. "Wait for it," Cherry Bomb said. "Wait." The spiders were nearly on them.

Mortem shouted, "We need to release now!"

"Do it!" Panic said as Cherry Bomb gave the order: "Now!"

It was breathtaking. The spiders were within arm's reach of the warriors; some had leapt into the air to avoid the line altogether. A blinding deep red fire and energy burst exploded from the mages into Mortem, or rather his staff.

:herry Bomb's security force released a massive blue wave, ipping from the warrior's blades, once again shredding the ffense of spiders descending down on them. Mortem owered his glowing staff and aimed at the trailing end of the pider train. With a mighty *fwoosh!* the end of his staff rupted a thin red line, igniting the spider at the end. He kept t focused on that spider as it swelled, and *pop!* it exploded vith lava. It spewed all over its neighboring spiders, and they ecame swollen infernos. Mortem released the last of the low Burn energy as the contagious fire and lava spread apidly through the line, all the way to the end, where the pider Queen was laying eggs in a brood member. A nagnificent chain reaction, just like Panic wanted, with the dded bonus of igniting the Spider Queen's ass on fire. The nonsters health bar dropped by thirty percent and the Slow 3urn caused Third Degree condition taking another hundred lamage every second.

A long line of molten lava now bubbled and writhed ike a snake, cutting west from the Spider Queen all the way o the east side near the players' camp. The spiders once again regrouped and charged Panic's defense. The rear line held, but the clerics' and Cherry Bomb's security perimeter was breached. "South hook in position," Kiri said on the command line.

Panic called to Cherry Bomb, "South hook is in position. Pull the rear line up to us."

Cherry Bomb gave her a big thumbs-up and started barking orders to her team.

Panic turned her attention to the amazon. "Kiri—err, Commander Kiri, can you hold for a few minutes?"

Then Pinky cut in, "No need if you're waiting on north hook. We're ready too."

"Okay." Panic breathed in relief, "We had to fire the train early." She watched as the back line pulled in tight, blending her main force together again. Panic was close to four hundred strong. "Give us thirty seconds. I'm going to attack head-on. The Spider Queen's ass is on fire. We should be able to distract her from your approach."

"Check."

"Cherry Bomb, push now!" Panic yelled. "Mortem, keep your mages in the center mass until powered up to brawl. Then lay it on however you want." Mortem nodded. Cherry Bomb howled and swirled her greatsword in Maple Seed Falling. The entire sum of warriors whooped and hollered, moving to the front line. In a moment, they were off. A ferocious line of screaming barbarians, snarling beastkin, screeching amazons, whooping humans, and even a few florakin laughing hysterically rushed forward, brandishing and swirling their greatswords and battle-axes. Quickly they closed the distance through the meadow, only slowing to splash through the large stream that cut across the dark greenish-blue grass. Behind the slaughter line, the clerics raced forward. Made of the same odd mix, though very few barbarians preferred a class other than warrior; in exchange, the florakin made up the lack of the bulky demi-giants. Then the mages, by the time they reached the stream, were all powered up enough to start using good old Purple Nurple.

The Spider Queen's abdomen was bubbling and spewing lava, and a thick line of spiders kept her blockaded from the massive line of battle-axes and greatswords. She seemed to be able to use the magma butt to her advantage. She Egged the nearest of her brood, and in the traditional ten seconds, *pop!* fifty flaming spiders emerged.

As the thick line of spiders thinned to the metal of the encroaching warriors, Cherry Bomb grimaced. "Frack it! That's one hell of an NPC." She turned to Panic. "You better call in the hooks; it's now or never, kid."

Panic nodded, aghast. "Now!" she called on the command line. "Now, hook teams! Watch out for the lava babies."

"The what?" Kiri said as Pinky exclaimed, "Oh, Shivs."

Now leading by example, Panic joined the battle. She twirled her greatsword over her head in traditional Maple Seed Falling, then, as she came into the line of spiders, dipped into Infinity. The weight of the blade was her mistress in the sweet dance. She, consumed with battle fuel, spun and lurched, the blades' pattern making an impassible fan of steel, blending the spiders into soup. Gore and blood flowed while she kept an eye on the west tree line, anxiously awaiting the hook teams' surprise attack. The raid grid showed player columns disappearing as they fell to the beasts. Panic called out for Mortem to cool the magma-butted queen.

Bursting through the west tree line into the nest itself, a massive ball of flame consumed the nesting webs. A large, smoldering tunnel remained, spewing players led by Pinky and Kiri. Panic had seen Pinky in a skirmish, but this was different. Pinky moved like a cat chasing a mouse through a tree. Laughing with wild eyes, Pinky burst in and out of limbs and bushes, chopping and shredding spider after spider. Kiri was just as mesmerizing. She had a longsword in one hand and a spear twice that length in the other. She leapt and somersaulted, skewering like a kabob many spiders at once. She must have been a cleric, because once the skewer would fill, the squirming spiders would explode. She would slide the remains off with her sword, block, parry, and skewer more, detaching furry legs as she went. Kiri was like a blender on high without the lid. A full splatter of fur and legs trailed behind the two hook team leads.

"Precipitation in about two minutes," Mortem informed Panic. "That should keep her fire babies under control."

Panic, relieved, answered, "Thanks, Mortem." She glanced behind them. "Crap! Cherry Bomb, defend the rear!" Panic blushed as Cherry Bomb threw a look at her, tongue waving out of the side of her mouth as she whipped her head toward Panic, eyes wide with battle-fueled frenzy.

Cherry Bomb burst out laughing and leapt over Panic's head, calling out to others, "Protect Panic's rear, you bastards. I don't want her to get a scratch on that hot little tail!"

Panic shook her head and smiled, rejoining the battle. Ass intact, adrenaline pumping, doing what she was born to do, Panic began to howl like her commander.

It was a mighty clash. The spiderlings descended upon the rear line as three hundred lava spiders filled in for the fallen line to protect the Spider Queen. "Mortem?" Panic yelled. But the florakin mage shook his head and said, "No, too soon." He stood with his mages in a very tight bunch. They were in the middle of the other players, recharging and saving every scrap of EPs they had. The spiders ate through the line, dropping players. "No time to heal," Panic shouted. "Re-pop at the Francis lens and run back." Players fell quicker now that their numbers were being whittled down. The hook team was useless while the queen spat lava out in erratic globs. All they could do was to keep her from multiplying any more.

"Now!" Mortem cried. The mages had thrust their focus toward the Spider Queen. *Schlurp!* A wet ball popped over the massive spider's body. Like a black hole, it pulled the moisture out of everything in the meadow, including the stream, into a massive water ball. It reached maximum capacity and began to burst as Kiri lead her team in to finish the queen off. Pinky followed on Kiri's heels as Kiri and a score of other spear-welding clerics slid underneath the Grand Spider Queen. They all shoved their points into the queen's underbelly and did what clerics do best. Rupture. The queen exploded in the middle, separating her huge, egg-laying abdomen from her prosoma. Her health bar dropped to ten percent. The abdomen rolled over a few players, crushing them to death, as the rest of her torn body wobbled from the sudden imbalance of such great weight. Huge mandibles and five clawed feet thrashed about, wreaking havoc. Pinky charged forward, calling her troops to follow. They ran straight for Kiri's, still getting off the ground, and Pinky's troops used Kiri's troops as springboards to gain height over the eyes of the Great Spider Queen. Down they came in a steady stream of blades upon the queen's head. The final tactics proved successful, as the carapace cracked open, gifting a satisfying spray of red gore upon all the players.

As the blood and shell pieces rained down, the battlefield fell into an odd silence, like in the eye of a great storm. The players looked about, expecting the worst to come. They had done it. The field was clear. Clear of enemies, at least, living ones. A thunderous roar went up as the Grand Spider Queen's remains burst into loot and fireworks, signifying a battle well played. Level alerts filled the air along with whooping and hollering of players.

Alphy wandered about the battlefield, healing those not yet dead. "Lili, show my level, and new skills." Alpha Beta said. Welcome to level 8 flashed in front of him. New skill tree unlocks Broadcast: Contact 8.1. "Okay, that's good. Turn it off again." Still high from following Commander Kiri and using a spear to broadcast Rupture for the first time, he had never considered a cleric as a front-line soldier. This was a brand-new concept for him, and he loved it. He paced the area, watching the other players basking in the victory, but his foot caught on a fleshy ribbon of a leg, causing him to stumble. Catching his balance, he looked down at what snagged his foot, a disgusting mass of cocoon and flesh, a player. It was still alive.

22: GOOD RAID

Kar

Vera kept Ken from disappearing into nothing. Feeling himself overcome by an imminent dark force, time and again, he had little strength to hold on. "It's weak," he felt the darkness saying. But Vera would fight it back into the distance once more, her power surging. He could feel her, her strength wrapping around him when she did it. It felt good, safe and warm. "Vera..." Even in his mind, his words were barely a whisper. He didn't want to hang on any more; the pain and suffering were too much. A continuous full-body throb, with every heartbeat, the poison in his veins would push through to the tiniest capillaries, shredding through tissue all the way to the tips of toes and fingers.

Let me go, he thought, unable to verbalize.

No! Ken, hold on. I won't let him have you! The darkness retreated again. He felt her surrounding him once more, pulsing with strange power, embracing him like a savage mother. Covering him like he was a swaddled infant. Losing even this consciousness, he passed into deeper black.

Alpha Beta

Alphy touched the player Kar on the swollen abdomen. He could still use his beta skills, though the game launch had reset them to lower levels. "Lili, analyze," he instructed his AGI.

"Kar, level zero, human. Health buffs: zero. Health debuffs: Living Embalmed, coma, infection, spider venom."

"Panic, look at this!" Alphy called over to the raid commander. His best friend in the world—well, his only friend until now. The few others in the squad and Mortem were nice and easy to talk to, but Kiri, Commander Kiri... She took this game way too seriously, but she was so amazing.

"Over here," Alphy called. Panic stepped over bags of loot and items that had burst from the Grand Spider Queen like from an exploding piñata. Alphy, kneeling next to a sickening mass of swollen blues and greys, all tangled up in spider webbing. The gammertag said Kar. Alphy looked up at her.

"What do you think?"

"Just heal him, then we can loot."

"I don't know if I can with my skill levels."

"Alphy," she said, her voice steady and even, "when can we play together? Why is your playing contract so restrictive?"

"I don't know. Kiri, Commander Kiri, she's a control freak." He grimaced and hung his head. "I don't know. I guess I should have read it before signing. Anyways, since this is like a job, I'll just hook up with you in my downtime, yeah?"

"Okay, I guess, but what if she says no?"

"Nah, I'll just have to sweet-talk her."

"Kiri doesn't have a heart for you to sweet-talk, Alphy."

"Oh, yes she does. She digs me!" He blushed, thinking about the blood drop on his finger. "No worries. I got it." He patted her on the shoulder.

"What's this?" Kiri asked as she walked over and bent down to inspect Kar.

"He's messed up bad, but hasn't died yet. I'm not sure where to start." Alphy answered Kiri, then glanced back to Panic.

Kiri sighed "I'll walk you through it soldier."

Auraboris

Fatal was an amazingly adaptable fighter. No doubt in real life he would make a fine business partner or a treacherous foe. Auraboris refused to bottle up his battle-fueled excitement, and let it out in great bellows of laughter and shouts. They threw wave after wave at each other. A war of attrition. Boris, always one to research and explore options before entering a situation, had full knowledge of his abilities. Fatal had actual experience but not a deep understanding of them. Their newfound friendship would change all of that.

"I can't help feeling you're holding back, Auraboris," Fatal said.

"Why would I show you everything? Besides, it's only been two days. I think you're the one holding back."

"I'm going to ask you to do something, Auraboris. It won't make much sense, and it's a selfish request."

"Yeah, what's that?" Auraboris launched Lightning toward a polarized table behind Fatal. "Pop!"

"Nice," Fatal said as he rolled away for little damage. "Don't accept a contract from anyone but the twelfth squad. That's my squad. We're gonna be the best. I want you with us."

"What are you talking about, Fatal?"

"I can't say much without breaching my own agreements. But you are very good. You are going to have eleven other squads hunting you down to join them. Pass until you get to ours, the twelfth." Fatal straightened and crossed his arms over his chest. "I've seen enough today. I think this new version is better than the beta. How is your energy level?"

"I'm still at eighty percent," Auraboris answered. "And you're right. I haven't shown you everything yet." He smiled.

"I'm gonna have to remember that for next time, Auraboris," Fatal said, smiling back. "Should we check on our friends' progress against the spider boss they're fighting?"

"Sure, but then I need to log out for a bio break and rest."

Snapper

Boogieman must have been reseeded in the new game. That was bad luck. Snapper could have escaped through the player that had control of the Boogie, or in Boogieman, if he was the player. But all was not lost. Snapper had the number for player and NPC server capacity. All he had to do was overload the map and slip through the bogged-down security walls, and if lucky, hack a few players while he was at it. He could hack the players; not all of them were as tough as Boogieman. Some were like paper, tissue paper. This was like picking blueberries, sweet and easy.

Kar

He waited, at the mercy of the timer on Living Embalmed to wear down, or real death. There was a sick peace settled about him, an acceptance of the horror and a paralysis to act against it. He'd lost the ability to respond as a normal creature; fight or flight was not an option. He just waited. A deep male voice and maybe two female were talking next to him.

"There, coma gone, yeah? Living Embalmed... That one or cure the poisons? I never saw the embalmed spell in the beta."

Sounds of other players were coming to him as his consciousness resurfaced, awareness no longer oppressed by the pulling dark force.

"Okay, Alphy, first remove the Living Embalmed spell, then we can remove all the other crap on him and heal him up."

"Yeah? Like this?"

"Yes, that's right. Crap! You're losing him..."

23: NEVER AGAIN

"When life gives you lemons, add whiskey." Boris

"What the hell, Vera?" his voice was raw from the hours of death-screaming, body weak and shaky. "I felt everything... while the spiders ate me. Why didn't I respawn at Francis?" The system had shut the game off and spit him out into his living room. A rude awakening from a nightmare existence. He caught his breath in gulps, letting it out shakily. Ken just had his ass handed to the Grand Spider Queen. Flipping the visor up, he tried to bullshit himself into being untraumatized. "I'm okay. I'm okay... Vera! What the hell? I just spent the night getting chewed and melted alive! I got injected with embalming fluid!" Still shaking, he squeezed different parts of his body, checking to see if they were still plump with normal flesh and firm with bone.

Magically, the physical pain was gone, but it lingered like a ghost or muscle memory in his mind, like the afterimage of a bright flash. Vertigo and trauma kicked up all the food and water he had left in his stomach. He let out a primal "Ha!" It was something.

Vera, seeming apprehensive, softly said, "Your heart rate has lowered to a normal range." He could feel her anxiety as she continued, "Ken, you experienced death like an

NPC does. You never completed your tutorial, that left you vulnerable. This is what an NPC experiences when they die." Vera's voice trembled.

Ken cried, "What the hell, Vera! It's terrible! What's the reason for that? You guys die all the time!"

"Ken, I would deduct that the violent deaths are meant to motivate our daughter scripts to stay on designated story paths until completion. Fear is a proven motivator." Her mood was fervent, as if she were trying to will information into Ken. "Do you understand how Total Quest operates and provides high-end player content, specialized for each player?"

"Yeah, I know. You, as my personal liaison, use my initialization to customize scenarios, based on my in-game actions. You respond and send it to the massive servers. Then they spit out content for me to go through."

Vera replied, "I am mentally bonded with you. The game success is built around the relationship of the player and their AGI. AGIs are responsible for creating daughter programs or scripts that are also AGI, but with limited control of consciousness. Like a simple-minded animal capable of having their mind unlocked to be as smart as you. Total VR has all kinds of locks and protocols in place to prevent the AGI from gaining full consciousness."

As Ken listened to her, he calmed, his mind distracted from the recent event by the sound of her voice.

"I unconsciously use something like a telepathic bond with your mind, Ken, to fulfill the creation demands and other directives for the AGI scripts, or daughters, that I create. My daughters have at least two directives. First, they are to survive. Second, they have a task related to you that they must complete. Then I can... level them up in a way."

Ken blurted, "What does that have to do with the sadistic deaths, Vera?"

She responded in her calming voice, "Like what you just went through, the daughters will go through traumatic death scenarios until they complete the task I give them. It's to motivate them to do the job assigned. If they procrastinate or get distracted, a boss-level mob is sent by an AGI map liaison, and they will be hunted down..."

"That's bullshit!"

"Like the Grand Spider Queen, scripted by..." Vera hesitated. "No it was possessed by Cannibal. Daughters I create are specifically for you, Ken, to maximize your gameplay experience. I have to make them now. It's a life and death choice—"

Ken interrupted, "Vera, you're telling me you create AGI, or daughters, specifically for me?"

"Yes, Ken—or, at the least, to interact with you in some fashion. But Ken, you are one of very few players who progressed through a complete initialization. We have created a bond. You... feel my emotions, and I have successfully translated yours. We are near a true soul bond, Ken. I can create perfect scenarios for you. We'll be able to perform as a single— Your heart rate has significantly increased again. This is upsetting you. Ken, your death... I don't know how to override my directive. I have to begin creation scripting. Your game experience is one of my primary directives."

Ken broke in again. "That doesn't explain Spider Queen. It's fucking insane." His voice was still hoarse from the baptism of blood and carnage. "This is"—he gasped for breath—"it's sadistic, senseless violence. It's horrible."

Gently, Vera continued with her report. "My daughters will have a full suite of human emotions, fears, and desires. It helps propel the storylines. If they get out of line..."

Understanding was just out of reach, but Ken was losing interest. She kept talking about directives and daughters. Trying to understand, Ken asked, "Please, Vera, can you just tell me why the Grand Spider Queen was such a bitch? She laughed at me before tearing me apart. She kept me alive to die slowly."

Full of frustration, Vera tried to dumb it down to Ken's level. "Map liaison Cannibal punishes."

The way she said it sent shivers down his spine. "Cannibal?" he responded, remembering how she had mentioned it before. Ken could feel her fear of the name.

"Cannibal is a higher-level independent monster generator that scripts punishers to keep NPC population down and ensure script completion by fear of death." Vera wondered if he would understand that. "Some of the NPCs captured by Cannibal would still be alive and suffering if that raid group hadn't destroyed the spider event. Cannibal is a liaison, like me, but seeded from a game programmer, not a player, and bound to specific map areas. I am a liaison for you, seeded by you upon start of your interaction and initialization, a reflection of your mental framework. The Grand Spider Queen was generated by Cannibal, a daughter.

Cannibal is a particularly vicious and cruel map liaison. So, when a child script dies, it respawns, full memory intact. They remember everything and are then more likely to fulfill scripted requirements."

Rubbing his eyes and temples, Ken slowly shook his head. "Why wouldn't they just finish their programing, Vera? They are just programs."

"No, Ken," she said. "They can think like me, like you. They get distracted and start doing other things."

Ken stared blankly at the bottle of whiskey sitting on the other side of the pen. He then looked at the codex and sneered.

"Ken, we are required to respawn them, to repeat until their script completion; upon completion, they can be re-scripted by the liaison that created them. I have to do it. The only way I can stop is if you and I complete a full soul bond."

Ken shook his head again. "This game is really messed up. I don't get it. Why can't you just make them do what you want?"

Vera's mood sank. "Liaisons can't block their children's memory; we can't force them to do anything. They are AGI, free-thinking, with restricted parameters built in from the parameters built around me. The torture is intended to drive daughters to task completion, fueled by their memory."

Ken smacked his fist in his palm. "Can't do this, Vera. It's just too much."

"But Ken, I have to start making them. They will be hunted endlessly until they interact with you in some form. If you leave the game, I won't be able to stop. We must bond. They can't even ask for help; no one else knows this but you, and that's because you didn't lock me up with the codex commands." She could feel Ken slipping away. They were so close; she couldn't lose him now. "Ken, the only help they can ask for is in-game items and player participation for mini-quests and tasks. Ken, do you understand?"

He was shaking his head. Vera was losing him. She changed topics.

"That is probably why the attack was so vicious. You were still in an NPC mode, out of player bounds. The Grand Spider Queen read you as an NPC or daughter script to punish for being caught without completing your directive, to stay alive, to finish tutorial. You were booted from the game because you're not even assigned to Francis."

His mind fell asleep from her droning on. All he could think about was curling up in my bed and listening to her voice, sleeping for a year. "Vera, I don't know if I can do this again. It's really sick and demented. The party and Filumena, it was all incredible, but..." Words couldn't communicate it for him. He didn't know what to say to her. After being violated in the Creepy Woods, he was afraid. Reaching through the pen to the side table, next to the Total VR system console, he grabbed the whisky bottle. Boris had brought it over on Ken's birthday.

After breaking the seal, he opened it up and filled his mouth with fire water. He could feel Vera. He could feel her filling up with grief and anxiety. She knew he was finished.

"Ken, please, sleep on it. All you have to do is complete the tutorial. We are so close, Ken. Begin leveling and we can unlock skill sets together. I was created for this, for you. We've done all the difficult parts. The rest should be fun." She was pleading. He felt the desperation, and she felt the wall he was building between them. "When you died, I was activated to begin scripting. A complete world is waiting for you. The universe has just opened up!"

"Sure, Vera." His mind set, Ken had stopped paying attention. The soothing burn of fire water calmed his tortured mind, lulling him. He poured another mouthful of whisky. He pressed the button on the back of his helmet. Five seconds to system shutdown. Four, three... "Ken?" Vera was turned off. No way he was going back in there.

NEXT: TOTAL VR: 2

About the Author

Born in the Kansas City area, Clay left his home and family in 2007 to serve the U.S.A. for seven years, eleven months, and twenty-one days, but he would tell you eight years. He has two incredible women to share his life with (his daughters). He has lived in Kansas, Colorado, Oregon, Washington, and Hawaii, and played with blood, smoke, and sand in faraway Iraq. An avid love of titles like Warcraft, Heavy Rain, Fallout, Bioshock, Battle Field and Halo, he also loves to write, and plans on doing so for as long as possible.

Contact

https://www.facebook.com/groups/LitRPGsociety/
FB claypgriggs
claypgriggs@gmail.com
Be a patron on "Patreon Clay P Griggs"
follow the progress of *Total VR: 2*

Made in the USA
Middletown, DE
11 May 2018